The Lynching Stream

By Horane Smith

PublishAmerica

Baltimore

First printing

ISBN: 1-59286-614-X
PUBLISHED BY PUBLISHAMERICA BOOK PUBLISHERS
www.publishamerica.com
Baltimore

Printed in the United States of America

Dedicated to the victims of lynching

"Blood on the leaves and blood at the root…"
Strange Fruit by Lewis Allen, sung by Billie Holiday

Chapter One

My grandmother's raspy voice boomed down the trail at me, triggering a reverberation that sliced through the early morning mist like an invisible intruder- an intruder that wanted to be heard.

"Luther! Come - breakfas' is ready…it's gonna get cold son," said the sturdy but aging voice as it echoed across the quiet valley from the small shack that was my home. Joyce Nesbeth was 70 years old, although her voice was not a real testament to her age. The voice rang in my ears for a few seconds and then it was swallowed by the silence of a new morning.

"Luther!"

The pleading voice begged again, waving goodbye to the serenity that I had been enjoying since I slipped from under my sheet to greet a new day. Grandma would call only twice. If I didn't respond, the coffee would get cold, and as for the cornbread, it would become husky and difficult to swallow.

Grandma and Kate, my younger sister, had been up from before daybreak baking that cornbread. We have been living with grandma from as long as I can remember.

I was sitting on a huge, flat rock, about fifty yards from the makeshift kitchen. Some mornings, I sat there until the sun crawled out of another world, and littered the valley with rays of gold. Me, I liked that. It showered me with an appreciation for nature, God, and the sanctity of life. It also gave me time to think.

This morning, I had been thinking a lot much about my father, more than I usually did. So much so that the thought of a warm cornbread and hot coffee simmering down my throat, did not stir my taste buds at all. Of late, questions, many questions, had started to tickle my brain.

I was only 28 years old. A descendant of African-American slaves who escaped to Canada through the Underground Railroad in 1855, my dark skin was symbolic of my enslaved American heritage and the struggle we have had to live with up to this very day: June 16, 1950.

I have a perfectly shaped face, with small dark brown 'penetrating' eyes that almost seem to carry a permanent sparkle. At least, that was how Grandma described me to my Uncle Bob, whom I met some years ago. Towering to nearly six feet, my lanky figure is ideal for my two hundred-pound weight.

Maybe I should pose this question to Grandma again – over coffee, of course. Grandma loved to watch me gulp down my steaming cup of her dark brew, relishing its flavor and the warmth it provided to my stomach.

"I thought you would neva' come," Grandma said, standing in the doorway.

I stepped passed her to take the coffee and cornbread that Kate was handing to me. Kate resembled me, according to Grandma. You could see the similarities especially when we were together. Kate was twenty five years old and about 5 ft. ten inches tall. She had a charming face, piercing eyes, and evenly placed lips that were tucked under her nose.

"I was going to have it y' know," Kate grinned teasingly.

"You could have it," I grinned back at her teasingly, "but all you would have to do is replace it."

"All the other mornings you jump at the sound o' ma call. This morning you pretend as if yuh is not hungry. What's the matter son?" Grandma asked, an inquiring face turning around to look at me.

I stared into her face, noticing the wrinkles around her eyes that appeared to be increasing each month. Age was catching up on Grandma slowly. Believe me, I desperately wanted her to enjoy her golden years.

Taking the food from her, I sat on an old wooden bench near the fireplace. Grandma took up her usual position beside me, while Kate sat on the bench beside her.

I sank my teeth into the soft and warm cornbread, the crispy sound making a crushing noise. "I am sure alright Grandma."

"That look son...ahem," she said, clearing her throat.

"What you talking 'bout grandma?" I asked, pausing before taking a bite into the cornbread.

"Something is on yuh mind. Yuh face is too innocent to deny guilt," Grandma said, sipping her coffee, placing the cup in her lap each time she took it from her mouth.

"Hmm, you don't want to hear it Grandma," I said, continuing to bite into the cornbread.

"I'm too old to have any further surprises in life son. Yuh might as well say it," she said with a grunt. I could see her eyebrows jerked a little pushing wrinkles into her forehead.

"Go on, say it!" Kate interjected, gesticulating with her hands as if she knew what I was going to say.

I stopped eating this time, and instead drank the remainder of the coffee. My eyes left my Grandmother's face and darted to the dusty floor of the kitchen. I had posed this question to Grandma before, in fact, on more than one occasion. She always refused to give an answer. According to her, the time was not yet befitting. I was wary that if something should happen to grandma at her age I would not get the answer to my question. That would always create a void in my life. As far as I was concerned, Grandma might be the only one with the answer. That was a hard pill to swallow.

"We know our father is dead. What we don't know is how he died?"

Grandma's face had a blank expression. A deafening silence followed. She looked like she had seen a ghost. She put the big coffee mug to her face and pretended to be drinking in order to hide her bewilderment. I theorized that the cup should have been empty by now. But grandma could not keep it there all morning. When she removed it, her expression revealed she was agitated by the question. Her face was serious as a judge, and there was not even the hint of a smirk.

Grandma should have guessed it was coming. The first time I asked that question was on my twenty-first birthday. It resurfaced on my twenty-fifth, and now this morning.

Did Grandma want us to know the truth? I could not say. Maybe she wanted us to know, and had been waiting on something I could not place a hand on. Grandma was persuaded she would not wake up one day; she believed she would die in her sleep: she always was adamant about that possibility.

Grandma had started to feel the effects of old age. She had served God all her life. One of the few remaining duties on earth was probably to tell her grandchildren the terrible truth about their father.

"Are you certain you want to hear?" Grandma knew the answer already. Nevertheless, she wanted that reassurance.

"I have been waiting anxiously for the past few years for that answer Grandma."

"How will that help yuh?" she asked, raising her eyebrows and nodding to indicate it wouldn't be of any help. She ran her fingers around the wrinkles on the lower part of her face. Nearly all of grandma's hair was covered with gray, typical of someone of her age. But she had the energy and drive of a middle-aged woman.

"That is left to be seen Grandma. The important thing is to know exactly what happened to our father. We know our mother died in childbirth...at least we should know how our father died," I said, finishing off the last bite of cornbread. That was a good thing, because I felt my appetite subsiding because of what I was about to hear.

"Kate, how do yuh feel about this?" grandma asked, turning her attention to Kate.

"I want to know, too, Grandma. Sometimes when I am at work I hear whispers and I have a feeling they might be talking about our father." Kate was a cook at Ashby's Restaurant on the outskirts of Sarnia, a border town in southwestern Ontario, Canada, near the Detroit border. We lived in Bakersfield, a small town about two miles from Sarnia.

"How yuh so certain about that?" she asked.

"I keep hearing the name Nesbeth. There aren't many Nesbeth's around here y'know."

"That's true. Suppose they ain't talking about yuh?"

"I don't think so. They are talking about a man. They keep referring to he."

"Yuh should be a lawyer," Grandma teased, revealing milky white teeth.

I looked at Grandma, wondering how long she would try to evade my question. How long would she keep us in suspense?

Suddenly, Grandma turned; I could hear the bench making a creaking sound with her shift in posture.

"Caleb Nesbeth was a good man, not because he was my son. Folks here know he worked hard to support his family. He had a difficult time making ends meet, especially after Kate was born. Times have been tough for our people."

Kate's eyes never left Grandmother's face. She was a good storyteller. I remember the harsh winters when we could hardly find enough to eat. Grandma kept us occupied with stories of slavery, and the Underground Railroad. We had to conserve a lot in order to make it through the grueling months of January and February, when the Canadian countryside is all plastered with white - as much as fifty inches of snow.

"Caleb decided to go to the mid-west to find work and send back money to take care of the family," she continued.

"He never made it?" I asked, anxious to hear the finale of the whole matter.

"He made it there. In fact, he started to work on a farm and then a store. Hmm, about a year later something terrible happened."

"What happened Grandma?" Kate asked, a perplexed look on her face.

I was puzzled, too. I became nervousness and began to shiver.

"He...they accused him of stabbing the store-owner he worked for in the town...Clarksville in Mississippi."

"Who accused him?" Kate asked.

I remained silent; all kind of ideas flowed through my mind.

"The folks who said they saw him. One day, a man claimed he went there, and found the owner bleeding from a stab wound. Caleb was standing over him with a knife. Yuh father was a kind man. Caleb told Uncle Bob he tried to press against his wound to stop the bleeding. The man said otherwise and ran to tell the sheriff. T-they arrested ...him." A tear crawled down Grandma's face, then another, until they came pouring down uncontrollably. She placed her hands over her mouth and wept bitterly.

It would be a moment I will never forget. To just sit there powerless and watch an elderly woman cry was no joy ride. I could feel anger even in my bones. All these years she had been living with this pain and grief. She did not speak of it to anyone; that must have made matters worse.

My disappointed self was open to all kinds of ideas and thoughts on how to react to this revelation. This was about my father – a father I never knew. One thing I knew for certain was that I was prepared to do something about his death. If it took the rest of my life to prove his innocence, right here and now, I decided I would channel all my energy into doing that.

Maybe I should have thought about it seriously before making such a impulsive decision. However, my dear old Grandmother was in pain. I was staring into her eyes and all I could see was anguish and grief. How on earth could I stand there and allow it go on just like that?

Surely, my Lord and Savior Jesus Christ would render whatever chastisement was due, if there was no repentance from those guilty of this terrible transgression. But my job was not about vindication. My job would be to exonerate my father.

Kate was crying too.

"Caleb didn't deserve that…," Grandma said painfully. "The next day…"

"Is he still in jail?" I asked timidly, fearful of the answer I would get. I told myself I had to know at all costs.

"My son…my son, that's why I have had to take care of yuh all these years. C-Caleb died…died the following day…"

"How?" I could hear my question ringing in Grandma's ear. This would be one of the most difficult times of her senior years. It was the question she had been wondering when to tell both of us. Kate and I knew mother died during childbirth. However, father's death remained a mystery.

I have heard many of the horror stories about the lynching of innocent men, especially black men, in several states. This had been going on for years, but not for one moment did I ever embrace the idea that it could happen to a member of my family. Up to this moment in my life, I have been assuming my father was tried and found guilty of murder and was subsequently executed by the state. Was there something else I should know?

Grandma turned away her head from them and gazed out into the early morning mist that had formed along the hillside - shades of white mixed with the dark green vegetation.

I followed her gaze and fixed my eyes on those hills recollecting the time we first settled here. There was not much to do and Kate and I spent a great deal of time setting booby traps for deer. The lush vegetation made it a worthwhile feeding ground for them.

The first trap we sat caught a raccoon instead. Three days later we hit the target – a fifty pound buck. That was the beginning of many successful hunts.

The smell of Grandma's venison stew on that first hunt would go with me to the grave. We filled our plates, and subsequently our palates, as often as we could for the ensuing days. It was one great feast that week with the full knowledge that come next week it could very well be famine.

I wondered whether Grandma was thinking about that too. But I doubted that - how to answer my question seemed to be the despicable burden.

Grandma turned her back to us. My ears itched for the unlikely and maybe horrible answer. Kate tried to relax, however, anxiety was getting the better part of her.

"He was lynched…taken out of the jail and lynched." Grandma grabbed onto the post beside her for support. She tried to suppress a sob but it slipped out. It was almost inaudible; it sounded like a diminishing trickle from a dying stream. I moved toward her. Kate followed, grabbing onto my hand. The three of us clung to each other, like the reunification of long lost relatives.

In the ensuing moments, I learned that tears respected no one – from the young to the old. I did not know I could cry – until that moment. I made no sounds: the tears took care of all the emotional outbursts. On the other hand, Kate's cries came with a loud scream. Grandma wept silently. Nevertheless, our tears found communal ground in that they were all shedding for the same cause.

My father was lynched by a mob of bloodthirsty people who weren't interested in a fair trial. My father never had a chance. Innocent blood was shed. He was black, that was no bonus.

We regained our composure and sat beside each other on the bench in the kitchen. We were barely saying anything, rather we allowed silence to speak for us. Now was not the opportune time to utter words that could aggravate our pain. We needed time to reflect. Me, I had already decided what my next move would be. No one else knew and I would wait on the appropriate time to disclose my intentions.

The sun was way above the hills now. The mist on the hillside had almost disappeared, except for that hanging further down the slope where the golden glow had not yet touched.

"I am going for a walk," I said. No one answered. "I will soon be back."

Kate and Grandma knew my solitary moments. There were many times when I preferred to be alone. I walked out of the kitchen.

"Are yuh going to work?" I heard Grandma asked Kate.

"It is better to go than stay here and feel sad," Kate replied. Kate's job took care of us well. Whatever she earned from it paid for food and other supplies that we needed, especially during the winter. The job was tough with long hours.

One good thing about the job was that the owner allowed her to take home food that was not sold. That came in very handy because grandma didn't have to prepare any dinner. Kate would take home some stew or fried chicken three days a week. So Grandma never cooked on those days.

I had no steady job to do. My job is to work the small plot of land that we have, to produce enough food for the coming winter. It was now August and the harvest was imminent.

I walked for about a mile until I came upon my favorite little stream winding its way down the hillside. Here, I did practically everything. This stream was life. Probably it would be till death do us part. I fished, bathed, did my laundry, fetched water for the animals and the plants, as well as domestic use. It was hard work.

Indeed, it was a beautiful morning. Nature was basking in all its glory: the variety of plants that formed part of the lush vegetation, the crystal clear water with small fishes jumping from side to side, the birds releasing melodies that couldn't be captured on a music sheet.

Oh! How I love this scene. It was my little world; providing solace, reminding me of my relationship with God; equipping me with reason to fight my inner battles and the ongoing struggle of war against my members daily.

I stooped at the side of the stream and scooped up some water in my hand. I placed it in my mouth, enjoying the cool sensation as it crawled down my throat. The water was pure, and according to Grandma, it could have some therapeutic properties. In her younger days, Grandma told me, every morning she walked to the stream to get that cup of cool and refreshing water. She attributed the daily sip to her freedom from any kind of stomach ailment.

I was far from superstitious. Nevertheless, should Grandma's theory be right, then I would be a benefactor. I was now repeating her practice.

Had my father been around, he would probably have some thoughts on that too. But then my father was no more. Since walking out here this morning, I had been trying to avoid thinking about him. However, everything I tried to think about, somehow my father got involved. There was no escaping that.

I looked at the stream and for a moment I thought he was there staring at me. My eyes reached for the trees, examining from the root to the slender bodies towering up into the sky. There was my father sitting on one of those sturdy limbs beckoning to me to come to him. I must be going crazy, I thought.

I sat on a rock bordering the side of the stream. As I sat down, I thought I heard a sound like clothes scraping against the rugged surface of the rock.

"It's okay," I said aloud. "Luther, you are not getting mad. You have a job to do and you are going to do it."

From the moment Grandma dropped the bombshell about my father, I knew a burden was placed on my shoulder. It would only be a matter of time before I had to take that first step. First step was to do what?

My father told his brother that he was innocent. That, I would prove; if it took me the rest of my lifetime then so be it. I was that determined.

Chapter Two

The shadows of the evening started to penetrate the walls of the kitchen. The surroundings had begun to take on the darkening effects of nocturnal splendor.

Nightfall is beautiful in Bakersfield. My stony seat near the house was not only confined to mornings. Some nights when the celestial bodies decorated the sky with their twinkling, glowing and shining, I would stare up above, sideways and ahead of me until my poor neck could no longer endure the discomfort.

I sat around the table in the kitchen looking at Kate at the other end. She was troubled. I did not need a doctor to convince me about that. Those dreamy eyes of hers told that story. They would not sleep tonight.

For more than half of the day, I sat on that rock near "Healing Stream," as I named it, wondering how she was reacting to the news from Grandma. Kate had left for work shortly after the disclosure and I didn't have time to talk to her about it.

Nevertheless, her initial reaction was vague. I remember searching her face for an expression and could not find any. That's Kate; throw your troubles on her and you may have to go somewhere else to hear how she is thinking.

My appetite was gone. The smell of Grandma's chicken soup played with my nose. But I was not interested in eating this afternoon. In fact, no one was eating.

The small table we use to sit around at dinnertime was as bare as could be. The pot with the soup remained on the fire, some coals glowing and flickering underneath it.

Grandma made no move to relieve the pot of some of its contents. The room was as quiet as the grave; the usually chatty dinner hour was absent this afternoon.

On most afternoons, Kate would lead off the conversation with what happened at work. Then I would follow with what I did in the field. Grandma would close it with a reflection on something spiritual, or preparing us to deal with problems in the future.

Somehow, this afternoon was different. And Grandma knew it. She wanted to change that but maybe she did not know how. She decided to break the silence.

"I know there's a lot to talk 'bout and to think 'bout," she said softly, with her hands clasped, "but please don't make it wear yuh down," she muttered slowly.

Kate didn't respond, neither did I.

"I was hoping neva' to have told both of yuh. It's hard for yuh. I know that. My children, a great burden is now off my mind. There is an expense to pay for that. There will be great pain."

I listened to her words carefully. There was wisdom in them. The forewarning should be heeded.

"You did the right thing, Grandma," Kate said quietly. "Please don't feel guilty about it. You did the right thing."

I guessed that it was now my turn to say something. I wanted to say the right thing, so in the few minutes that I had before the words would leave my lips, my thinking cap was working double time.

"I agree. You did the right thing Grandma," I said with sincerity.

"Will it change anything?" Grandma asked.

I did not expect such a question from her. I could see she had been thinking about it all day.

Kate looked at me. The impression I got was that she wanted me to answer her question. There was no doubt that I should be the one - after all my mind had been preoccupied with my father's fate all day.

My mind was already made up. There was hardly anyone who could change that. I did not know how to tell them my decision.

The sudden presence of someone standing in the narrow doorway tested my reflexes. I passed the test. I wondered how long the person was standing there and might have been listening to our conversation. This was a family matter, or to be more precise, a family secret.

Lena Kingsley was no stranger to the family, or to me. She was our next door neighbor, and my very good friend. Sometimes I tend to believe we had more than friendship going. At this time, I didn't know whether she should be hearing the conversation.

Lena was a beautiful girl of twenty-five years old. Her round face was perfect for her body. Those eyes of hers would be ideal for performing hypnosis, especially if the patients were of the opposite sex. Her dark skin was without blemish; that added to her undeniably attractiveness. Lena wore a permanent smile that made you wonder if she ever had sad moments.

"It is no longer a secret," Lena said, smiling with everyone.

Kate and grandma turned to the direction of the voice. "Hi my dear, come right in," Grandma told her.

"I hope I am not intruding."

"Yuh is like family," Grandma replied.

"How long have you been standing there?" I was forced to ask.

"Uh-huh, spying on me eh?" Lena said, with hands akimbo and coming to sit beside me.

"Not really. I just didn't see you," I managed to say, trying to hide the true intent of my question.

"I am invisible whenever I want to be," Lena laughed.

"Have something to eat?" Grandma asked. I could see she wanted to use the opportunity to get everyone to eat now, despite our reluctance to do so.

"I am okay Miss Joyce, I had dinner already."

"How was work today?" Kate asked, speaking up for the first time since she came in. Lena worked as a janitor at the local elementary school. It was a good paying job enabling her to help take care of the family - mother and two younger sisters.

We were the only colored families living in the area so we were very close.

"It was busy as usual. How about you?"

"I was busy too. I didn't even have time to think," Kate said.

"That's better especially when you have something bothering you. How about you?" she asked, looking at me.

"I was busy all day too."

"Doing the usual I suppose," Lena assumed.

I started to get a feeling she was searching for information. Lena must have caught a piece of our conversation and knew something was wrong. If it affected me, she felt it concerned her too.

"Doing the usual," I assured her. "The potatoes, carrots, broccoli, squash and the rest are long in the ground. We have been blessed with timely showers and all I can do is wait for the harvest."

"That is a nice way to put it," Grandma said.

"School is out for me soon and summer is here," Lena said. "I want to take a trip south."

Lena had told me that the last time we spoke. She was adamant about spending some time with her relatives in Bloomington, Mississippi. My father was lynched in the same state. That was where my mind was at this time. I don't know how far away Clarksville was from Bloomington. The fact that I was thinking of the same state was enough reason to give serious thought to my plans.

The moon came out with a boldness that was unmatched in the heavens. It spread silvery rays on trees, rocks, houses, and on Lena and me. We were sitting on my favorite seat – the rock.

The lone light from the window in the house was still wavering away. It was nearly eight o'clock. Both Grandma and Kate were preparing for dreamland.

Sleep was far away from me. I had too many things on my mind.

Lena didn't make it a point of duty to stay out here with me most of the time she came. Tonight was different. Something was amiss.

"It's so nice out here. It's a pity we don't have nights like this all year round. I am already dreading winter. That's why I would have wanted to go south during the winter," Lena said.

"What would you do about your job?"

"That's the reason why I want to go next month."

"I may be joining you...er, well not joining but going to that state too," I said, watching closely for her reaction. I couldn't see those eyes in the moonlight but I did see a startled and bewildered look on her face.

"What do you mean?"

"I have business to do in Clarksville."

"Is Clarksville in Mississippi?"

"It is but don't ask me exactly where."

"If you don't mind me asking, what business do you have down there?"

"It is a long story," I said, knowing she would be prodding me for some answers.

"That was what you were discussing this evening."

"As a matter of fact, you are fortunate to know this before them," I told her.

"Hmm, that is interesting. You didn't answer the question."

I searched her face in the moonlight. The outline only reflected its attractive features. While I sat there admiring them, I tried to figure out her insistence in learning more about the conversation with Grandma. Yes, she was always like that. However, from all indications she was not giving up on this one.

"I don't know if it would be of any value to you," I said playing with my fingers.

Lena placed her hand over mine. "I believe the time has come for both of us to put away our shyness. We should be more open with each other and have no secrets."

"I agree," was all I could say.

"We are no longer teenagers Luther. We are mature adults. I was hoping you would discourage me from going south. I know you are to shy to do that, right?"

"I agree," I said again.

"What I am trying to say, Luther, is that seeing we have more than just ordinary friendship…you would agree," she said, stopping in mid sentence to get my reaction.

I nodded, too shy to answer, or blushing at her proposition.

"Then it stands to reason that what will affect you would affect me. Something is going on Luther, something I believe I deserve to know."

I could have listened to her talk all night. After all, I could not have spelled it out clearly, as she was doing tonight.

"I came to tell you this morning that I have finally decided to go south for the holidays to get your reaction…to hear from your lips a plea from you not to go. You were not around."

I could hear disappointment in her tone. Perhaps, there was a voice crying out for something which I could not give or know how to give. I was embarrassed.

"Miss Joyce told me you went down by the river. I was late for work. That didn't matter. I had to see you. When I saw your face looking into that water, I knew something was wrong. That was not the Luther I know. Are you ready to tell me now?" Lena asked, squeezing my hand tighter.

So I was not going insane after all. I remembered that sound. Nevertheless, I was trapped. Lena had finally spelled it out about our undefined relationship. I had to thank her for giving the proper definition now. At least, it saved me the trouble.

As she talked a few minutes ago, I had begun to realize that I owed her a lot of respect. Lena had earned that and she deserved it too.

"Why didn't you join me?" I asked her. That was not something I would have wanted. Regardless of that, I wanted to show care and concern for her.

"It could have been awkward for you. I thought about it and then decided it would be best to leave you alone."

"Sometimes a little company can be good. Y'know you get these moments and you cannot handle them alone. Two heads are better than one, you know what I mean."

Lena chuckled. She kept looking ahead of her away from my range of sight and undoubtedly Lena had some moments of regret. I was interested to know what she had been thinking in that regard.

"How long will you be gone for?" she asked.

"That is a good question. The answer is I honestly don't know."

"Maybe I should not have said what I just did. It makes no sense now," Lena said, her head remaining in the same position.

I wanted to believe tears were in those eyes. On the other hand, I would have preferred if they were not. Why? I did not know how I would handle the situation. "I don't understand."

Lena placed her hand on her chin as if she was trying to keep her head steady. I was convinced she was crying.

My heart raced a beat. My skin started to itch; and I could feel a slight headache coming on. In one quick instant, I did something I never did before in my entire life. I thought it was the right thing to do. I edged closer to Lena, placed my hand around her shoulder and started to hug her. She turned and started to cuddle up against me. Then there was a huge sob followed by another, and another, until they were too numerous to count.

I tried to comfort her, not wanting Lena to wake up Kate and Grandma. Lena calmed down after a rather long minute had elapsed.

"Everything will be fine," I told her. I wanted Lena to believe that although it was only a wish on my part. "This is about my father…"

Lena withdrew from my grip. Suddenly, all traces of crying vanished into the darkness and she was back to her true self. "What do you mean?" she asked, nodding her head in disbelief. "What is going on Luther?"

I had to tell her. "Grandma told us this morning that our father was lynched for a crime he did not commit."

"What! How?" She rose from her seat, both hands resting on her head. Lena was about to explode again.

I reached for her quickly and started to hug her once again. "Please don't cry…please don't cry. I don't want you to wake Grandma and put her through this agony again," I begged Lena.

As soon as I said that, I felt something wet soaking through my shirt. Lena's head was resting on my chest and the silent cry poured out more tears in the dark than I could have imagined.

My eyes were glazed; although the tears were building up, I would not cry – at least not yet. I held her for a few minutes and when I presumed she had stopped crying, I released my hold on her.

We took back up our seating positions and were speechless for a while. It would be better for Lena to say something.

She did. "Why are you going?"

"The only time I am going to be satisfied is to bring justice…to prove his innocence. It will be difficult. There is no denying that. I am determined as ever and that is why I must do this for my father and for me."

"Where will you begin?"

"Clarksville. That's why I am going there."

"You need some help. Where will you get help?" Lena asked, sounding doubtful about the whole venture.

"I have an uncle in Clarksville...Uncle Bob. That's all I know. If he can't help, I will find it somewhere else. All I need is to get a job. I am a good hand at anything, and farm work could provide what I need."

"Hmm. You will be leaving Miss Joyce, eh?"

I hated to think about that. I had been avoiding that question since I made my decision. The question was staring me in the face now; it was best that I deal with it here and now.

"I have every confidence that Kate can manage until I get back. Furthermore, you and Mrs. Kingsley are around." Lena lost her father last year following a short illness.

"When are you going to tell Miss Joyce?"

"Tomorrow. I want to leave this weekend and return in time for the harvest," I said confidently.

"Do you think that's possible? What could you learn in three months?"

"Enough for me to take the matter to the authorities."

"How do you expect me to survive without you all this time?" Lena asked, holding my hand.

"It will be difficult for both of us Lena. Please remember one thing, I am coming back..."

"I am telling you now that I will help with the harvest if you don't come back on time. I will help take care of Miss Joyce, too," Lena said. I had no time to resist, even if I wanted to do that. Lena made one step closer and hugged me again – this time tighter.

On Saturday morning, I did not rise from my slumber at my usual hour. I was too exhausted, not physically, but certainly mentally. For most of the night, as I had been doing for the past two nights, I had been going through my plans for leaving Bakersfield.

How would I prove my father's innocence? I was not a lawyer, had no knowledge of the law whatsoever, except I know you should not kill, steal or hurt someone. I had to admit my plans were a bit fuzzy; maybe the anxiety to leave had taken away any ability I had to make some concrete plans.

Time was running out. Each day that went by Grandma was getting older. The earlier I could leave would be the better. If I go now, I could be back before next summer. My only concern now was about the harvest although Lena had promised to take over its care until my return.

I rose from my bed feebly. Kate and Grandma watched me stagger into the kitchen. Apparently, they already had something to eat.

Grandma handed me a steaming cup of coffee and a thick slice of bread plastered with butter; the latter I know came from the restaurant. My teeth sank into the bread grinding it mercilessly. They watched me in awe as I minced it into a kind of wet powder.

"I can see yuh appetite is back," grandma said after I took the last gulp of coffee.

I couldn't deny that I had lost it for a few days. "Hmm, I guess you are right."

"It's time to move on son. We cannot live in the past."

Now was the time, I told myself. Any other time would be more difficult. "I know you are not going to like what you are going to hear Grandma…but please understand that this is something I have to do."

Grandma looked me straight in the eyes. Already, she seemed to be saying no to what she had not yet been told. Kate looked on, too, wanting to say something. I continued quickly, preventing her from making my job even more difficult.

"I have to go to Clarksville, " I said softly, waiting for a reaction before I continued. Both faces were expressionless maybe anticipating more information before reacting.

"This has been bothering me. Now that we know the circumstances of our father's death, there is no way I can stay here and do nothing about it. I will do it if it's the last thing I do before I die. I have to prove my father's innocence. Grandma and Kate, I hate to leave you both but please understand this is something I have to do."

A mosquito buzzed around the room; the only sound you could

hear in the uneasy calm that followed my statement. I could not see the mosquito, although I wanted to get up and put an end to its annoying sound.

My eyes blinked in a struggle to focus on the elusive menace. The agony associated with defeat was coming over me as I failed to detect its trail.

The mosquito moved away from me when I buckled my arm and flashed my hand beside my ear. It was Grandma's turn; she, too, slapped at the insect. I heard a retreating buzz and then it was no more. Grandma's hand had found its target.

With the mosquito now out of the way, I couldn't figure out what Kate was thinking. Grandma appeared somber, and yet in a not so obvious manner, she seemed either pleased or proud with my decision. "When will yuh leave?" she asked timidly.

"In a few days. If I can, I would very much like to return before winter. Lena has promised to help with the harvest, if I don't get back in time. Can you both manage?" I was very concerned about that.

"We can Luther. We have to manage…this is very important to us. If yuh have to, please go without delay. My poor father…" Kate's hand went over her face and she started to cry.

Grandma placed her hand around Kate trying to comfort her. "Luther is doing the right thing child. Caleb…a dear son, it is such a pity yuh both didn't get to know the wonderful man who fathered yuh. Go with Jesus an' he will walk with yuh every step along the way son."

Those words would forever ring in my ears. I stood there feeling somewhat relieved that they, too, were thinking like me. What more could I want?

"Thank you Grandma. Those words mean a lot to me."

"Yuh Uncle Bob will be happy to see yuh. I can tell you he will go all the way with yuh on this. He wanted to do that long ago for his brother. Now he has the help he needs."

"I have everything worked out already Grandma and you don't have to worry about anything."

I went over to sit beside Grandma and Kate and all three of us joined in one embrace. Tears started to flow from the three pairs of eyes. We weren't sure whether those were tears of joy or tears of sorrow.

Somehow, I thought of my little stream flowing below me. The sound of running water was beckoning to me to row on to a new land and to return with tears of joy. I wished it was all that simple.

Chapter Three

The sound of metal against metal was loud enough to inform me it was time to move. It was time to leave Sarnia; it was time to leave Bakersfield. Mississippi, here I come.

The huge freight train I was sitting in would pull out of Sarnia within minutes. Then it would move into Port Huron, Michigan – a new country and one I have never visited before.

I am a Canadian citizen and an American as well because of my mother's place of birth. Nevertheless, in a matter of minutes, I would be a stranger to this new land in search of justice. I was trying to correct a wrong done to my father and the countless others, who had been lynched innocently, since the latter part of the nineteenth century.

I had to do this smartly. I had to play detective. I had to play my cards right. Thank God for that lucrative harvest last year, and that we were able to save some money; I was able to take a portion with me now. That could serve me for the time I decided to stay in Clarksville.

It was almost midnight. The next freight train was set to leave Sarnia at midnight. According to the information that Kate was able to glean from the people who delivered goods at the restaurant she worked, this train would pass through St. Louis, Missouri. From St Louis, I would have to take another one to Kansas City. From there, I should have no problem getting to Bakersfield.

I was not a passenger on this train. For one, it was not a passenger train. It was carrying cargo and I was only hitching a ride in an unceremonious way. That seemed to be the only way.

I had crouched in the far corner of the penultimate coach for two hours now. My shield was several bags of beans. They were stacked from floor to ceiling, except for one shorter row near the corner where I was able to hide myself from any crew inspection.

My goodbye ordeal had begun around 6 o'clock. Grandma, Kate

and Lena had gathered at the house to see me off. At first, I got the impression that it was going to be a simple goodbye.

We had started to exchange pleasantries. We prayed, joked about being caught during the journey and about my becoming some kind of a hero because I was able to prove the innocence of Caleb Nesbeth.

Everything was okay up to that point. However, when I started to take up my bag, all three women rushed me in one grand hug. Within seconds, it was like a sea of grief. Sobs mixed with tears soon turned into open crying. My challenge was not to join them. I walked over slowly, my feet wobbling as if they were going to give way.

We clung to each other for a while, not saying anything or making another step. I felt I had to make one last speech before I ventured into the unknown.

"I know you may all be wondering when I am going to come back," I said, recovering from what had just transpired. "Believe me, I don't intend to spend a great deal of time in Clarksville. I know what I am going there for and I don't have time to waste. I have to take care of you all," I said, remembering my efforts to force a smile.

The sound of voices disrupted my thoughts. I eased up out of my crouching position and peeped through the open spaces between the board of the coach. The rail yard was lit brightly. Doors were banging loudly indicating that the coaches were being checked.

My eyes tried to comb as wide an angle as I could. Voices were coming closer and closer; the bodies behind them were nowhere to be seen.

Tension rippled through my body. My skin itched and a slight headache started in the center of my forehead. There was silence again. Maybe they had stopped the inspection. I kept looking out for about two minutes – nothing.

Having satisfied myself that the inspection might have been confined to one coach, I slumped back into my sitting position listening anxiously for the sound of the whistle to signal departure time.

Suddenly, there was a yank on the door of my coach. It was flung open in a split second. Light from the station beamed inside the coach illuminating my dark corner with a glare enough to be discovered.

At nightfall, I had made my way into the coach without any problems. The door was half opened. However, an hour after that a crew member came and slammed it so hard I couldn't hear for a while.

"Can this coach take anymore?" someone asked.

"I don't think so. I checked it already," another voice said.

"Are you certain about that? I am almost sure there was some space in that corner over there."

"I can look again, if you want."

My heart pounded against my chest as if it was going to burst through the flesh, and tumbled to the floor. They had to be talking about my corner.

"It's alright, I take your word on it," the other voice replied.

"Thank God," I whispered to myself.

I remained seated until I heard the door slam shut again. I placed my hands over my ears to shield the loudness. The voices faded into whispers the further they walked away from the coach.

Two other coaches were checked, and then about half an hour later, the gigantic piece of moving steel pulled out of the city.

Clarksville, here comes trouble, I said to myself. The murderers of my father prepare to meet his offspring – a determined young man who will not stop until true justice is meted out to the perpetrators of this injustice.

Yesterday, Lena handed me something I never thought of receiving. It was a small package with some newspaper clippings from the school library – all about the lynching of innocent people in the United States. The vast majority of them were colored people.

Grandma made a commitment to Kate and I, shortly after our father's death. "You will learn to read and write," she told us one day while she was reading her Bible. "We suffer too much when we cannot read or write."

Those newspapers provided the education I needed about the horror of lynching. I was appalled at the number of lynching.

First, I learned that lynching had been around for a while. In fact, it began in post-Civil War America, shortly after Reconstruction – a time to reunite the country in the transition from slavery to freedom.

Lawlessness and the lack of an adequate judicial system led to mob violence. Some chose to take the laws into their own hands, as they lost faith that criminals would be truly punished for their crimes. However, the executions failed to distinguish between the innocent and the guilty.

From 1882 to 1930, the same year my father was lynched, there were nearly 3,500 victims. In 1892 alone, there were some 230,161 coloreds and 39 whites. The lynching were in several states but many occurred in the Deep South.

Tears came to my eyes when I read that men who were innocent, and sometimes women, were tortured and dismembered before they were killed. There were reports of creating a kind of festivity with regard to the executions. Some people had the gall to treat them as a sport by buying tickets to places where lynching would be carried out. To make matters worse, some parts of the victims were kept as souvenirs.

I could not imagine my father's fingers, or a toe, for that matter being chopped off and being kept somewhere as a souvenir. Anger burned the walls of my stomach and I felt more compelled now to fulfill my mission. I felt truly bitter, yet I reminded myself not to allow my ire to meddle with what I hope to achieve.

The sound of the whistle I had been anticipating pierced the night air like a call to battle. It was the sweetest sound I had heard in a long time.

The train jerked and the huge iron wheels rubbed against the rail line igniting sparks of fire, and a caustic odor of burning metal. Up ahead, the exhaust from the engine puffed dark smoke into the black sky. The driver in the engine room shouted to his colleagues in the adjoining coach, and then the train slowly moved out of its dormant position.

It picked up speed by the minute, and before I knew it, Lake St. Clair and Lake Huron were behind me. Soon after, the fading lights of Sarnia and Port Huron disappeared into blackness and I realized I was now in the United States. Having come this far, my eyes were telling me it was time to get some sleep.

It was the sparkling rays of the sun that stirred me up next morning. I jumped to my feet and looked between the slits of the coach to see the sun way up in the sky. It was almost mid morning.

I must have been very tired because all that jerking and winding did not wake me all night. I could have easily been found without even any warning.

My bag was with me and it contains all that I need for the next few days. I have no choice but to ration whatever food I have with me – freshly baked cornbread, apples, dried beef, dried fish, corn cakes and a few other items.

I munched on a piece of cornbread and drank some water. My thoughts raced back to home. Grandma must be at home thinking all sorts of possibilities. As for Kate and Lena, they had started to count the days I would be away.

Clarksville was still far away. Nevertheless, I began to formulate a strategy to clear my father's name. I knew from the beginning that it was not going to be easy. However, it was time now to begin to think exactly how I would do that.

The train seemed it would keep going on and on. It stopped at quite a few big cities, the names of which I could not tell. All I knew was during those stops, especially at nights, I opened the door to the coach and carefully pushed it back in order not to close it, and then made use of whatever toilet facilities were available.

At the end of the third day, I was perilously close to running out of food. Fortunately, I found a bakery at one of those stops and bought some hot bread and butter.

The baker, a tall slim man in his sixties, hesitated at first when he heard my order. My theory was that he wondered if I would have been able to pay for it, or he didn't want to serve me because of the color of my skin.

Another man who was also ordering bread eyed me cautiously as if

I was an escaped convict or something, and kept doing so even when he was on his way out. I got my order and hurried through parked trains, and abandoned cars and made my way back to my "little home." I made sure I was not being followed or noticed.

As nightfall came over this vast land known as the United States, my journey was ending its fourth day and entering its fifth. St. Louis came into view shortly before midnight. On the last stop before that, I heard talk close to my coach that St. Louis would be the next stop.

The train pulled into St. Louis whistling and hooting as if in celebration of a mission accomplished. I hopped off as soon as the screeching brakes forced those tall iron wheels to come to a halt.

The rail yard was huge, much bigger than the one in Sarnia. I didn't know where to go, or where to find east, west, north or south. But what I could see ahead brought an element of delight to my worried mind.

However, there could be a problem. Two men were walking towards me and that stopped me in my tracks. My delight in seeing four parked trains on the other side of station was short-lived.

The light shining on their caps told me they were railway workers. They must have seen me coming out of the coach. I tried to slip into the shadows but it was too late. They walked faster towards me and were almost within reach.

"Whoa, what are you doing here?" one of them said in a very rough and coarse voice.

"Nuthing suh," I managed to blurt out of my trembling lips.

"Nuthing?" he echoed, in a kind of teasing way.

"Were you riding on this train?" the other man asked, trying to see me clearly in the shadows.

"Y-Yes suh."

"Who told you to do such a thing? Do you know how many people have died or been punished for doing that boy?"

"No suh."

"Too numerous to mention. Where are you going?"

"Mississippi suh. Clarksville."

"Hmm. That is a place with a reputation. What are you doing in that place? You could get lynched," he joked.

The word lynched rang in my ears. All of a sudden, I was frightened. Frightened by the prospect of being lynched innocently as happened to my father.

Of course this man was joking. Suppose his joke could truly become a reality for me? I became paranoid and began to think of all the remote possibilities as likely to happen to me. Since I left Sarnia, paranoia had been plaguing me in my dreams and now in my consciousness.

The man was waiting for an answer. I didn't know what they were up to at this hour of the night. They could easily do anything that came to mind.

"I have relatives in Clarkesville suh."

"And you are looking for another train to take you there eh boy?" the one who first spoke said with a grin.

Both of them looked at me, as if to say, admit it or we are going to do something to you. What should I do good Lord? What would you have done in this situation Dear God? You would have told the truth. I know that and decide to do just that.

"Yes suh. I have no other way of getting there."

Neither of the men said anything for the next thirty seconds. I feared their next move. My knees could have been knocking against each other. If they were, I was not aware of it. Sweat trickled down my spine even though the night was rather cool. I could feel it slipping down my back stealthily.

The men exchanged glances. I could see that in the dark. What was going through their minds? I wondered. God, everything is in your hands, I said to myself.

"Where are your parents?" he asked.

"They are dead suh," I replied.

"Huh, that doesn't sound too good. Who do you have in Clarkesville?"

"My uncle suh."

"You are going to spend some time eh?"

"Yes suh."

The man scratched the side of his face. "You appear to be a good boy, eh."

Prayer answered. That was my immediate reaction.

"We shouldn't be doing this," the man continued, measuring me down from head to toe, "but because you seem to be a good boy, we are going to help."

"I don't know how to thank you suh," I said smiling in the dark.

"We whites are not always evil. That is a thought to begin with, right?'

I nodded.

"That train over there," he said pointing to the same train I had my eyes on a few minutes ago, "it leaves for Kansas City in half an hour. Take the last coach or you will have to wait for another day or two. Clarkesville will be your fourth stop."

"Oh Dear God thank you so much," I said aloud this time. I truly meant that. As for the men, I dropped my bag and grabbed them by the shoulder not waiting for them to extend their hands.

"Thank yuh… I thank you very much in Jesus' name."

I sailed past them without even waiting for an answer. When I looked back, their heads were turned towards me watching my trek toward the train.

I remember Grandma always tells me: when someone gives a positive answer about an important matter act on it before the person changes his or her mind. That was exactly what I did just now.

With that assurance from the two railway workers, I opened the door of the coach in the manner of a paying passenger. Inside was dark as expected and the cargo was once again beans and some other grain.

I looked back through the door out into the dark. I could not see whether the men were out there. My next move was to pull up the door of the coach and wait for the train to begin its journey into Mississippi.

I did not know what happened next. All I knew was some time in the wee hours of the morning, I jumped out of my sleep after being awakened by a loud squeaking noise. I could not remember when the train left Bakersfield.

The train had stopped. I could hear voices up at the front of the train. Fifteen minutes went by and then there was a jerk again and the train moved off.

By late afternoon the next day, the train had already cleared its second stop. There was no need to get off, so I remained inside and walked around to stretch my muscles. Two down, two more to go.

The other two stops came quicker than the first two. The big surprise I got was the big sign staring at me at the fourth stop. It said "Bakersfield," and I couldn't be happier. Had I known that the sign was there, I would have been more relaxed.

It was broad daylight and my desire to sneak out of the coach was not going to be possible. This cargo could be bound for Bakersfield. With no intention of taking any chances, I watched the few passers by and when the opportune time came I jumped to the ground quickly and pretended to walk as if nothing out of the ordinary had taken place.

The township of Bakersfield was right beside the railway station. It was a beautiful town. A river wormed its way right through the heart of the town and continued its way into infinity.

Grandma told me Uncle Bob lived on Milton Street, four blocks north of Main Street. That should not be so difficult to find.

I walked up Main Street and it was as busy as a bee. It appeared to be an ordinary town – white folks, and a few coloreds, stores, cars, and all the other things one could expect in a town.

No one noticed me and I was kind of happy with that. I smiled to myself and mused that maybe in another few weeks this town could be noticing me because of what I was about to do.

Chapter Four

Uncle Bob lived at 45 Milton Street, exactly as Grandma said. I don't remember Grandma mentioning whether he had a family or not. Uncle Bob lived alone in a small shack at the end of the street.

All the houses on the street looked like Uncle Bob's. I had started to wonder if it was the trend in this section of town. From all indications, I was right.

Uncle Bob would be getting the shock of his life. He didn't know I was coming, and undoubtedly this would be a surprise visit. I had promised to visit some time, but I don't think he was expecting me today.

I tapped on the door and it opened almost immediately. I needed no spectacles to see that this was Grandma's son. Hard times were taking their toll on Uncle Bob. I could see that in his face. For a man of about fifty, my father's younger brother, Uncle Bob gave you the impression that he was about sixty-five or so.

He had a wiry face; tinges of gray dotted the sides of his head, and his face had wrinkles around the mouth and eyes.

Grandma's features were evident in his face. Those eyes, the thick lips, and that rather fleshy nose. Did my father bear any resemblance? There was no picture of him of which I could tell. Hence, it was my conclusion I would never get to know. That troubled me.

Uncle Bob looked me over, and when recognition came to his mind his face erupted in a smile that stretched from one side of his face to the other.

"By golly, ain't this a surprise. Look at you!" he backed off in order to examine me, "If this ain't Caleb's own self. Mama has been feeding yuh good son. Caleb would have been proud of you," Uncle Bob said grabbing me by the shoulder.

35

I couldn't help but notice how often he mentioned my father's name. "Thanks Uncle Bob. That's very kind of you."

Uncle Bob's expression changed quickly, and he was no longer smiling. "Is Mama okay?" he asked abruptly.

"Oh yes, she's fine. Everything is fine," I assured him, knowing that he was concerned that my presence might mean bad news.

"Oh. I didn't expect to see you…at least not now. Here, let me take your bag. This is my humble home. It ain't a palace neither is it a garbage dump. The important thing is it provides shelter; when the rains come there's no leak. You are invited to stay as long as you want. Did ya eat?"

"I could do well with a hot meal. I traveled on the train all the way here feeding on cold and stale food," I said, anxious to have something warm in my stomach.

"Is that so? Well, you will like my stew made fresh as the garden green," he chuckled.

Uncle Bob had a sense of humor that I was beginning to like. My father never had that opportunity to show me that so maybe Uncle Bob would try to make up for it.

"You didn't go to work today?" I asked.

"I don't work on Saturdays," he said simply.

"Saturday? Oh! I lost track of the days. Traveling in those coaches was really an experience."

"You is a brave young man to come all the way here in a coach. Tell me about my mamma sir. Is she keeping up that well?"

"Grandma is as strong as a lion. She doesn't get sick and she works all day. I'm not worried about her. Kate is taking good care of her."

"Kate, hmm, the last time I saw her she was a little girl. She must be a grown woman now," Uncle Bob nodded.

"She is…she works at a restaurant as a cook and she takes good care of us. I work my little farm just to feed us."

"Good boy. I am a farmer myself. Lately I help some white folks nearby to run their store. I don't have a lot of land so that helps me out with my living expenses."

"Life is tough out here, eh?"

36

"Yes son. I cannot hide that. Sometimes I wish I was with you up there in Canada. I'm alone here. I have been hanging on all these years…"

"Hoping to prove my father's innocence?"

Uncle Bob's eyes went from my face down to his clasped hand resting on the table. I turned away my head unable to look at the expression on his face. I could hear the disappointment in his voice. I pitied him.

"And that's why you are here," he said slowly.

I nodded.

"I am glad you came because I ain't doing nuthing 'bout it. I am more concerned 'bout my survival than finding the culprits of such a horrible crime. I'm ashamed of myself son. I'm so ashamed. Please forgive me," Uncle Bob said, hanging his head to avoid my glance.

"There's nothing to forgive you for."

"Caleb and I came together to work here. Now he is gone all these years. I know that he didn't do no stabbing and yet he was lynched for that. Son, you cannot imagine how I feel. It has been restless nights and days living in agony. That's the punishment I have to pay for doing nuthing all these years."

It's a rather awkward moment for anyone to watch a grown man shed tears. Right before me was my dear uncle, a very humble man - a man who would do anything for his family. But there was a sense of hopelessness here; Uncle Bob wanted to do something about his shortcomings; the harsh reality was he didn't have the guts to do it.

"We're going to do it together Uncle Bob…beginning on Monday, we start our investigation to find out who was responsible for my father's lynching."

Uncle Bob's face lit up; he started to smile again. "You truly mean that?"

"I do, with all of my heart I do Uncle Bob," I said, clenching my fist.

"Heh! Heh! Heh! You have made my day son," he said, getting up from his seat. He walked over to the fireplace and return with a steaming pot of stew and two plates.

"Let's eat and be merry because we don't know what tomorrow may bring. It could be something bad, it could be something good," he laughed.

I was very happy that I was able to cheer him up. "Let's focus on the latter Uncle Bob."

"I agree son," he nodded.

Admittedly, I like the use of his term "son." After all, as far as I know, he does not have any children. As far as I am concerned, I have never had anyone calling me son. I have to get use to the idea because over the next few months, I will be living under his roof.

We ate in silence for a few minutes. "Are you interested in any work while you are here?" Uncle Bob asked.

"I wouldn't mind doing that as long as it doesn't prevent me from doing what I am here for."

"William P. Pearsley & Sons is the big store in this town. The Pearsleys own one of the general stores, the only hotel, the drug store, and I believe the gas station. I work with them most of the time," Uncle Bob said.

"What do you do there?" I asked curiously.

"Everything. I work in the store, sometimes at the gas station and any little errand they want me to do. A.T. Pearsley and his brother Jacob is the owners and his daughter and granddaughter actually run the businesses. Mr. Pearsley is getting old. Would you be interested?"

"Maybe," I shrugged. On second thoughts, I believe the experience would be good for me. "Is the pay good?"

"Son, this is America. This is Mississippi, a segregated state. Slavery has been abolished, but we still work for little or nothing. What can we do? We have to eat. Only God can rescue us; the politicians don't even care. We need a voice for our people, a strong voice like Booker T. Washington."

"Do you go to church?" I asked, wondering if he was as close to the church as Grandma.

"Every Sunday son; tomorrow is included too," he hinted with almost a laugh.

"I'll be there. We always go every Sunday."

"We have no hope in this life so why not think about the life to come. America is so rich and we the people who help to build this country is so poor. Some of us live worst than pigs! It's hopeless for us son," he said angrily.

I glanced through the window. I saw a group of children, all colored, skipping along the road merrily. "What is life like around here anyway?"

"Life is simple. People mind their own business, especially the colored folks. We work hard to earn our wages to feed our families, go to church, praise God, and await our day with death. That's life in a nutshell, nothing much to it," he assured me.

"Tell me about Dad's death," I said. Obviously, I startled Uncle Bob. I could see that.

"Are you ready for it?" he asked, looking away from me while scratching his unkempt beard.

"More than ever," I replied.

My first night in Bakersfield left me sleepless. I thought I would fall asleep quickly, given my tireless journey from Canada. Not so, I would have fallen asleep all right, however, Uncle Bob's explanation kept me thinking. Uncle Bob was very short on details. I could see why he wasn't able to do much.

According to him, within the space of two days everything was done and over with.

The black folks in the town were denied any information about the circumstances leading up to the lynching, as well as what happened at the lynching. All he could say was Caleb didn't come home one night. Desperate for information, Uncle Bob made several inquiries around town. No one was interested in saying anything.

However, Rebecca Pearson, the daughter of A.T. Pearsley, told him in secret that my father was at the jail in town. He was allegedly found standing with a knife in his hand over a bleeding businessman the evening before.

Caleb was arrested with attempted murder. Uncle Bob said he pleaded and begged to see him. He was refused repeatedly. He insisted on sleeping in front of the jail for as long as he was there. Sheriff Hank Kerrigan decided he would give him five minutes on the condition that Uncle Bob never returned to see him.

Uncle Bob didn't have much of a choice. He opted to see him far from being convinced that he had done the right thing.

Uncle Bob said my father never stopped crying. In the little time that he had, my father told him to take a message to Grandma. The message was; "I did not stab the man. I saw him bleeding and went over to help him."

That was all. Uncle Bob promised to get a lawyer for him, although my father said he shouldn't bother because he had someone who came on the scene and would testify in his defense. My father was confident that his ordeal would soon be over and done with in a few days.

Unfortunately, that was not so. Uncle Bob did his regular job at the store, went home to get a good night's rest, being comforted with the thought that everything would turn out just fine.

The next morning, Uncle Bob said, was the worst day of his life. His watery eyes confirmed my worst fear; my father was lynched the same night.

Uncle Bob dramatized how the early next morning he heard a thud on his door. Trembling, he managed to reach the door, opened it, and was greeted with the presence of my father – dead. His still warm body slumped there motionlessly. There was no one around.

Uncle Bob was saddled with the burden of preparing for the burial of an innocent man – my father, his brother. Once again, Rebecca came to his rescue by helping with the expenses for the funeral.

Uncle Bob said he couldn't work for nearly a month. He was so overtaken with grief and shock that he couldn't concentrate on what he was doing.

Those were the thoughts that bombarded my mind now. How could I sleep after hearing such an episode? I got up during the night and went out to the small kitchen.

Uncle Bob stirred beside me when I slipped from under the sheet. I tiptoed in order not to wake him. It didn't make any sense.

"Go on, I can't sleep either," I heard his voice behind me.

"Ugh, I…do you have any tea?" I muttered softly.

"Oh yes, I have the famous one from…Ceylon, I believe. Very expensive and taste very good," he chuckled.

"Can you afford that?" I turned around to ask him, as he turned on the lamp.

"Miss Dorothy gave it to me as a reward for helping her clean up her flower garden."

"Who's Miss Dorothy?"

"She is Rebecca's daughter. They are good people. I don't know how I could do without them. You will meet them on Monday morning."

"I'm looking forward to meeting them."

"Troubled about what I told you eh?" Uncle Bob was on his feet now.

"You should get some sleep," I said, meaning what I had said.

"I'm not going to work tomorrow. I have all night y'know. If I'm sleeping in church I'm depending on you to wake me," he teased.

"I will." I wanted to ask a question. How would Uncle Bob react was of concern to me. I honestly didn't want to cause him anymore pain. However, the reality is that as long as I am in Bakersfield, the question will come up sooner or later.

"Where is Dad buried Uncle Bob? I owe it to him and Grandma to visit."

Surprisingly, he took it quite good. "In fact, I was planning to take you over there tomorrow. I may well pass by Rebecca and pick up my Sunday dinner," he grinned sheepishly.

I joined him at the table. It was obvious that this Rebecca meant a lot to Uncle Bob. I started thinking about that for a while, wondering how it could affect my investigation. "What is it with this Rebecca?" I asked, regrets on my lips as soon as I finished the question.

Should I have asked such a question? Suppose there was something, though unlikely, going on between them? I could be intruding.

"Ha! Ha! Ha! Son…they are good people, they care for me. She is always reminding me that anytime I don't have Sunday dinner, please come by."

"That's interesting. I'm looking forward to meeting them," I said, having two minds about such a meeting.

"You'll like her, especially Dorothy. She's one helluva young woman."

"Hmm, if she can be of help that's all I want to know."

"Rebecca knows something but I never get the guts to ask her about it," Uncle Bob said.

"About my father? Has she said anything to you about that?" I asked, anticipating a positive answer.

Uncle Bob tried to yawn while speaking at the same time. "Not in so many words. From time to time, she refers back to the days when they took lynching as a hobby. She never gave details only expressed remorse, if you can call it that."

"Who are they?" I asked, noticing this word was coming up a little more than usual.

"Those responsible," he said flatly.

"But who are they? Is there any of them in this town? If they are, this is where we have to start," I said a little excitement building up in my voice. I was behaving as if I was onto something already.

"Listen son, we have to be cautious about our approach," he said, gesticulating with his finger.

"No one must know, understand?" I wanted that assurance from Uncle Bob because in the long run, it could be very important in arriving at a verdict.

"I understand perfectly…that's what I have been trying to do all these years."

"Good. Who was the businessman that was stabbed?"

"Mr. Hays. I don't even remember his first name," Uncle Bob said with ease.

"Where is he now?" I asked, sleep now far, far, away from me.

"All they would tell me was he opened a business in another town. Nothing else, no matter how I tried, my pleas fell on deaf ears," he said convincingly.

"And the sheriff."

"Don't ever talk about him. Sheriff Kerrigan had no backbone. He is retired now."

"Is that business in operation now?"

"From what I know, the Barkers, Tim Barker and Jacob Pearsley have a drug store there now."

"This is getting more interesting Uncle Bob. Our job isn't going to be easy. Prepare to spend long nights with me examining all kinds of possibilities."

"I am prepared son, very well prepared."

Bakersfield was sprinkled with the golden rays of the sun on the day named after the fiery star. There was not a cloud to greet the sky. It was one beautiful day to give praise to the Creator for his handiwork.

We walked to the church about five blocks away. The church was a small building capable of holding maybe a hundred people. When I peeped inside there was no doubt that more than that number was there – all colored folks.

We were right on time. As soon as we were seated, the resonating voices from the choir rumbled across the valley. The members sang their hearts out in a unified and sweet melody that was not lacking in tenor, soprano, alto, or bass.

After a few brief introductions, we went to where my father was buried. I stood about six feet away from the tomb before going right up to it. For a moment, it didn't make sense to me that his remains were so near to me. After so many years, I had finally seen his resting place. My eyes were glossy with tears. I wanted to say something aloud; the courage was not there. I searched for words; they seemed to run out of my head.

We stayed there for a few minutes, not saying anything. I couldn't imagine my father lying six feet under the cold ground all because of a false accusation. Deep down in my mind I told myself that this mission had to be a success.

We left the burial ground with watery eyes. Uncle Bob said he was going by Rebecca's for dinner. Rebecca lived on the outskirts of town, the riverbank bordering her backyard. It was a nice place, neatly tucked away in a zone where not many houses were situated. She could have all the breathing space she needed.

I learned from Uncle Bob that Rebecca lost her husband when Dorothy was only three years old. He died in a boating accident on the Mississippi River.

Rebecca was a rather cute looking woman. A blonde with blue eyes and a face ready to smile; she had her hair in a ponytail that made her look even younger than her forty or so years. She was medium-built, with a very soft voice.

"Bob, is this Luther that you speak about sometimes?" she asked as we met her in the pathway leading up to her house. She was watering the flowers along the hedges lining the pathway.

A figure burst from around the corner of the house at full speed. With a bucket of water in hand, the person almost ended up bouncing into me. I made one step backward in order to avoid a collision. It was a girl; her face changed color, either in fright or anger, when she realized what was about to happen. I reached out calmly and grabbed her by the hand to prevent her from falling. Her arm almost got twisted in the process but somehow I followed her movements and was able to prevent that from happening.

"Ohhhhhh, I am going…I am going to fall," she screamed. Uncle Bob and Rebecca watched her helplessly. By now, they could see easily that I was the only one in a position to help her.

"You'll be okay," I said, on the verge of laughing.

"You think it's funny?" she yelled.

I held her hand until she was standing firmly. The bucket with the water was empty. She looked at it in disbelief.

"Thank you," she said embarrassed, as it dawned on her that I was the one responsible for preventing her fall.

"Oh, thank you er…"

"Luther," I said.

Uncle Bob made two steps forward. "By the way, that was a show of skill…Dorothy, this is the nephew I'm always speaking about."

"So here you are in the flesh," Dorothy said, biting her lips.

"It's a pleasure to meet you Luther," Rebecca said. "Your uncle never stops talking about you and we never thought we would get to meet you."

"I'm glad to be here ma'am."

"How long will you be here for?" Dorothy asked, retrieving the bucket.

"For as long as I'm needed," I said with a laugh.

"Bob, dinner is almost ready. You are right on time. Let's go right inside," Rebecca said, pointing to the way.

Rebecca's dining and living rooms were situated neatly into one big space. There was ample space to accommodate both rooms. The furniture wasn't anything out of the ordinary; they seemed to fit in well with the blend of colors from the curtains, tablecloth, and rug.

Dorothy's eyes never left me since that mishap. It was noticeable to me although I didn't know whether the others were aware of that. At times, she scrutinized me from the corner of her eyes and at other times she looked at me directly. I simply had to pretend that I was not conscious of her stare.

While the table was being set for dinner, I sat there with Uncle Bob watching the two women moving to and from the kitchen. My thoughts were not on their movements; I was deeply in thought wondering where to begin my mission.

Information was so scanty; everyone involved had been tight-lipped over the years. From what I could glean, the information regarding my father was confined to a small circle of friends and conspirators. The identity of those people was a closely guarded secret. My challenge had become more formidable by this conclusion. Yes, I would like to be right on that. At the same time, I feared my mission could end in failure, or it could take a much longer time than I had anticipated. That was the last thing I wanted to do.

For one, I know Grandma was counting the days and so was Kate. As for Lena, I know she was drafting plans for our future. I could take pleasure in knowing there were people back in Canada, who cared about me and the success of my mission. That was enough to keep me going.

"Dinner is ready," Rebecca announced.

I could hardly wait. My stomach was growling in discomfort because of the absence of food. We had nothing to eat since we left for church. The services lasted for what appeared to be a lengthy two hours; we had been here for nearly an hour.

The smell of Rebecca's roast beef tempted my nose. Suddenly, my mouth was full with water. It was a relief when she asked Uncle Bob to grace the table.

My mind was so preoccupied with the smell of food that I didn't even notice that Dorothy had decided to sit beside me. Whether it was deliberate, or not, I could not say. All I could say at this stage was that her eyes once again had resumed their search on me. I must have blushed a thousand times. If I kept blushing at this rate, then sooner or later it would mean nothing to me.

However, my immediate concern now was food. My hunger had robbed me of my ability to distinguish between good and bad cooking. If one should judge by aroma, then the huge slab of beef before me, the baked potatoes, the gravy and the steamed vegetables would be at the top of their class in taste.

My teeth sank into a slice of beef accompanied by potatoes; my suspicion was confirmed. The food was delicious. They must have noticed my indulgence in fulfilling a commitment to my stomach. I ate in silence.

Dorothy must have been observing my preoccupation with the food. I couldn't help it because I didn't realize the extent of my hunger until now.

My stomach was noticing the difference between empty and almost full. Gradually my mouth began to chew slower and slower until it wasn't chewing at all. I placed my fork down only to notice that the others were continuing to eat. Their pace had been much slower and their plates had a lot on them to be devoured.

"That was quick," Dorothy said, a warm smile turned into a laugh.

"I was starving. It has been a long day," I managed to mumble.

"Eat more if you want," Rebecca said.

"Thanks. I am full. I couldn't take a spoonful more. That was good ma'am."

"Thank you. Any Sunday you want to come over, please do so. You don't need an invitation."

I tried not to look at Dorothy. I knew her eyes were fixed on me, there was no need to turn my attention in that direction.

After dinner was over, we sat in the living room and talked about life in Mississippi. We must have been there for about an hour.

"Do you want me to show you around?" Dorothy asked me.

There was no way I could say no to such an invitation. "That is a good idea," I said.

Uncle Bob and Rebecca both smiled as they watched us depart from their presence.

We walked around the house and out to the back of the premises. A river ran by and then disappeared into the forest.

"This is the Blue River, a tributary of the great Mississippi."

"I am sorry to learn about your father."

"The Mississippi took him from us. Life has never been the same for us, especially Ma."

"It must have been tough."

"It has been tough in the sense that he is not around. My Grandfather takes care of us very well. He is a wealthy man. Is your father alive?" she asked, leaning her head as she posed that question.

"No, I lost my father too. I don't remember him," I said with care and caution. Apparently, Uncle Bob did not tell them Caleb was my father. That was good for me if I were to get information from whatever source was available.

"How did he die?" Dorothy asked, the questions coming at me like they were coming from a lawyer.

"It's been a mystery. Some day I hope to get the answer."

"Is your mother alive?"

I thought Uncle Bob would have given them those details. Maybe he had a good reason not to, and if that was it, then I had no objections to that.

"She died before my father. She died in childbirth," I said calmly.

"How sad? So who took care of you?" she asked, taking a seat on a tree stump beside the river.

I sat down adjacent to her, picked up a twig, and started to draw some lines in the sand at my feet.

"My dear Grandmother. She has been mother and father to me, and my sister Kate. We cannot repay her for that. Right now, I know she must be worried about me."

"Why? Can't you take care of yourself?"

I laughed. "Of course I can. She doesn't expect me to hang around here for long."

"How long do you intend to stay here for?" Dorothy was a very attractive girl. Already, I had started to admire the way her chin protruded from under her mouth, giving her face the attention it deserved from curious eyes. Her mouth was not small, neither was it big. It was perfect. The fact that it could easily break into a smile made Dorothy an eye catcher.

On top of that, her egg-shaped face was surrounded by shoulder length hair. Yes, Dorothy was one of those rare beauties that one would meet but don't get close enough to in order become friends. Instantaneously, I reminded myself that America was not ready for inter-racial relationships. I had learned from one of those newspaper stories on lynching that inter-racial marriage was illegal in Mississippi. If a colored man was charged for rape, lynching was seen as the likely answer .The few that existed do so under secrecy.

My blood ran cold; my thoughts raced back to another of those newspaper articles Lena gave me in Canada. It was the story of Jesse Washington, a seventeen- year-old colored youth that was lynched in 1916, in Waco, Texas, in the most horrible, gruesome, and inhumane manner one could ever perceive.

The report said he was stripped of his clothes, dipped into coal oil, hoisted into a tree, then lowered into a fire below. Some of the estimated fifteen thousand cheering spectators gathered for the "festive occasion" removed his fingers and toes for souvenirs.

The youth was found guilty of murdering a white woman, after confessing to the crime. He was condemned to hang, but a mob snatched him out of the City Court five minutes after the sentencing.

To make matters worse, the remains of Washington were put in a bag and hung from a pole for passers by to see. Post cards were made of the hanging. I felt nauseous in my stomach.

"Is something wrong?" Dorothy asked.

I could not answer her right away. The thought of getting too involved with her and the consequences of such an idiotic move gave me something to think about. A colored man could not win, should there be any harm whatsoever to a white woman, a pretty one at that. This was 1950's America and the battle for civil rights was yet to be won. In fact, it might have just begun.

The problems we face in Canada are maybe not as bad as here in America. Nevertheless, we had them to deal with too, although not with the fervor and passion as we see starting here. Poor Kate has been confined to do all the cleaning up in the kitchen where she works. That's all she could get to do. Her job helps a great deal especially during the winter when we cannot grow anything. As for me, I remember being told once that I could not enter a hotel, and in another case, a restaurant. Grandma could tell countless stories of the problems she faced in Canada because of her color.

I could not hide my nervousness just sitting here with Dorothy. Jesse Washington's horror story would serve as a guide for me from here onwards. I had no intention of committing any murder against any person, be they black or white. Any crime whatsoever against society could be punishable by death. As a black man, that thought must sink into and register in my psyche at all times.

"I think we should go," I said, not wanting to continue the conversation.

"Did I say something wrong?" Dorothy asked. She was concerned, that I could see with ease.

"Oh! No! I'm a bit tired and sleepy, that's all."

"You provide good company. I was about to use this opportunity to get to know you better," she remarked.

"I'm sorry," I replied.

We walked back to the house almost in silence. The few words we exchanged were about the nice weather. To my relief, when we stepped back into the house Uncle Bob was ready to go.

"It's been a long day son. I hope you is ready," Uncle Bob greeted me in the living room. He was already standing, an indication that he was rearing to go.

"I am."

"Did you two have a good time?" Rebecca poked in.

Dorothy responded quickly. "It was well worth it Ma. I find Luther to be a very interesting person."

I wasn't expecting that compliment. Instead of saying anything, I smiled and nodded my head in approval. So much for the hypocrisy; I could not stay there much longer. I honestly wanted to go.

"Do come to see us again Luther?" Rebecca said.

"Anytime you want," Dorothy interjected.

"I was planning to take Luther with me tomorrow to see if there's any little work around the store that he could do while he's here," Uncle Bob suggested.

I was hoping that Uncle Bob would have shelved that idea for a while. Although I did not say anything to him in that regard, I needed time to clear my clouded mind from all the thoughts that were now entering it – the latest being Dorothy.

Dorothy's face radiated with that suggestion from Uncle Bob. She smiled broadly, then turned to her mother to await her response.

"I don't believe that would be a problem Bob. There's always something to do around the store. You can come tomorrow if you wish Luther," Rebecca said, directing her answer to me.

"Thank you very much ma'am," I said, putting no thought into my answer. I was glad I replied in that manner. She was doing me a favor. However, I wondered why on earth would she do that for me.

Chapter Five

Early Monday morning, Uncle Bob and I were the first to be at A.T. Pearsley's. At least, so we thought. We were standing outside the main door waiting for Rebecca to come to open the huge steel bar at the entrance.

That said door was flung open from behind us. Rebecca and Dorothy stood there almost laughing for surprising us.

"Hmm, we thought we was early, " Uncle Bob said.

"We beat you to it this morning," Dorothy replied.

"Well, let's get this store ready for the customers," Rebecca said, handing me a broom that was in a nearby corner. "Your first chore here," she smiled.

That was good enough for me. I stepped past Dorothy and started my new job. Dorothy's eyes were all over me. The most I could do was to pretend I was not aware of that.

Lunchtime came quicker than I thought. I had been busy all morning packing, sorting out goods, as well as getting the storeroom in a presentable manner.

"I can't believe it!" Rebecca said, when she walked in shortly before midday. "Bob has been wanting to do that for some time now; here you are doing it better than anybody else could have done. Thanks a lot for a job well done."

"Thanks ma'am. I was only trying to do my best," I replied, trying to humble myself with that compliment.

Uncle Bob was not around lunchtime. Rebecca told me he was on an errand a few blocks away. She gave me a cheese sandwich, telling me to take my lunch break.

Dorothy was busy at the counter. I decided not to hang around until she got her break. I decided to go for a walk. My feet carried me across the bridge at the end of Main Street, then to an open lot beside the road. The open lot turned out to be a playground of some sort.

Some trees formed a neat row along the edge of the lot. I walked over there; my ears picked up the sound of running water. I could not have missed that for a thousand dollars. It reminded me so much of my little stream back home.

It was there all right. Indeed, a stream winding through curves and rocks and vegetation, made its way along the side of the playground. The playground, maybe a small baseball field, was flat except for the northern edge that tapered off into the stream. It was shallow at some points, but could have been up to four feet in depth at other spots. The stream was about ten feet wide at one section where it broaden its flow at the root of a huge oak tree. That tree made a huge difference to the stream back home.

My ears responded in delight at the sound of the running water. Oh! how I liked to hear that. That brought back so much memory of life in Canada.

I searched diligently around the vicinity of the stream to find a rock. I knew I could not find any like the one in Bakersfield. When I did find one it was not as big, moreover not as smooth as the one back home. Nevertheless, it would make do for as long as I was going to be in Clarksville. I found a flat surface and sat there as if I was in Canada.

Some birds chirped away in the tree above. It must have been about a dozen of them. The melodies that they were spewing out sounded like a disorganized symphony.

My eyes tried to pick them out of the branches; not even one came into view.

"They sing like that every day," a soft voice said.

I turned at the sound of the voice. It was Dorothy. She stood there, the sun glistening on her brown hair putting her in the league of someone from fairyland. She had a small bag in her hand; I didn't have to ask what she was doing here. My guess was twofold: lunch or a familiarization visit.

"Ugh, you startled me," I admitted.

"What are you doing here? I didn't expect to see you," she said, coming to sit beside me.

My heart pounded against my chest. This was a public place; what would be the reaction if we were seen together. Of course, segregation in America is real and better not discussed.

"You come here often?" I asked, my eyes searching the entire compound to see if we had company. There was no one.

"I come here almost everyday for lunch. This place carries a lot of memories for me."

"Hmm, my lunch break is over so I think I better go," I said getting up.

"Come on, hang on a few more minutes. Ma is taking care of everything back there."

"Did Uncle get back before you left?" I asked.

"No, I don't think he'll be back until this afternoon."

"What's this place called?"

"It is called Cold Stream."

"Cold Stream? Why Cold Stream? The water isn't cold, is it?" I stepped close to the sides and scooped up some of the water. Truly, it was cold, not too cold, but cold. "You are right."

"It's very cool out here this time of the year. As winter draws nearer it gets colder. You are from the colder East. I am assuming you are used to that kind of weather."

"I am. I have a little stream near my house that reminds me so much of this one."

"Ha! Cold Stream is incomparable to any other," Dorothy laughed.

"Why?"

"That's a long story. It's been around long before I was born. I see you are ready to go."

I nodded, hoping she would not be walking back with me.

"Go on. I will soon be there."

"See you later," I replied, quite relieved to get away from her.

On my way back, I kept looking around at the faces of the town. The people were mostly middle-aged and upward. I must have seen about two other colored faces during my walk. They beckoned to me, while about three of the other folks, stared me in the face and moved on.

Uncle Bob was in a contemplative mood tonight. Supper was over and we were relaxing after a busy day. I could see he was tired and wanted some time to reflect on whatever was on his mind. At least, that was what I thought.

"How was your day son?" he asked, raising his head from his pillow in the couch.

"I cannot complain. I was so busy that I didn't even know when it was time to go home," I responded.

"I'm glad to hear that. I was hurrying to reach back in time for lunch but I couldn't make it. Where did you go?"

"I went by Cold Stream."

"Cold Stream?" he asked, a little surprised.

"Yes, Cold Stream."

"How did you know about that so quickly?" he asked wide-eyed.

"I went for a walk and ended up there. While I was there I saw Dorothy came by for lunch."

"Hmm, that's her favorite place. That is a memorable place son. It is very popular nowadays...very quiet and relaxing. I want to tell you though...son you have to be very careful in this town. You know what I mean?"

"I know what you are talking about. Be careful with Dorothy right?" I said, raising my eyebrows.

"Yes son, be careful of everyone that is not of your color. We are still segregated. Serious friendship with white people is a serious crime...very serious."

"I know."

Some are reasonable people. There are some that would hope you disappear from the face of the earth. If they ever know why you are here that would only makes matters worse," Uncle Bob said, studying my face.

"The other night when we were talking you mentioned a possible witness to the incident involving my father and the businessman."

"Hmm," Uncle Bob said, rubbing his jaw, "yes, I hear there was a witness. All these years I have been trying to find that witness. Son, it's a mystery. It's either the witness has been paid to keep quiet, or the witness is as cold blooded as the people responsible for lynching your father."

"Who told you there was a witness?"

"Rebecca, of course. She has been the source of most of my information."

"Has she been helping you to find that witness?" I asked, getting more and more interested in the relationship between my uncle and Rebecca.

"Rebecca told me once that she would try. In fact, on more than one occasion she told me to give her some time. I know it must be difficult for her. My good friend Benny Harris keeps telling me not to pressure her too much because she may lose interest."

"Where is Benny?"

"He lives at the end of the street. You will soon meet him and his daughter. I was hoping to see them at church yesterday."

"How much does Benny know about what happened?" I was beginning to wonder when would I get to meet the colored folks in Clarkesville.

"Son, the colored people in this town don't know a thing. I understand there was another lynching here in 1915, and unlike Caleb's, it was not a cover up. It was very public because people came from far to witness it. I also understand one of the poor man's fingers was cut off by the main instigator for a souvenir," he said, flashing his hand in disgust.

"My feeling is that something went terribly wrong with my father's murder. That's why much information isn't around. Do you believe it has all been forgotten after so many years?" I wondered about that now, because lynching was on the decline nowadays.

"I believe they have all forgotten that now. The younger ones don't care about history; the older ones, I believe, will carry that to their graves. They don't talk about it," Uncle Bob shrugged, " but that doesn't mean they have forgotten it. That's too much of a horrible stain on their past. I wouldn't be surprised son if they have nightmares every night," he said, taking some comfort in saying that.

With that, I decided to get some sleep.

We left for work at the usual time. I didn't know if it was because Uncle Bob was talking about nightmares last night that I was plagued with them throughout my sleep. They came one after the other and they all involved my father. In my dreams, my father was angry that the authorities had done nothing to avenge his innocence.

I was troubled. Yes, the dreams were not real. However, the way I was feeling indicated that I unconsciously accepted them for reality.

Once again, my first chore was to sweep the store. I didn't hesitate about doing that. Uncle Bob proceeded to the back to finish stocking away some tin goods. I grabbed my broom and started at the floor.

Rebecca and Dorothy were behind the counter preparing for the day's sales. I didn't see anyone come in; what greeted my ear was a gruff voice that I never heard before.

"Don't flash that broom too hard boy or else the dust will go on the goods. You be careful you hear me boy?"

I turned around in a flash. An elderly white-haired man was standing only about a yard away. He was dressed all in white – the cane he was carrying was white, so was the hat on his head.

The eyes were as blue as could be; the face couldn't take any more wrinkles. The hawk nose was perched on a face that could have been that of a handsome man, yet the face had aged too much now to figure out what it was like in the past.

There was a striking resemblance between the man I was looking at, and the figure behind the counter. Rebecca's features, particularly the eyes, told me this had to be her father A.T. Pearsley. Another man, a rubber stamp of Mr. Pearsley walked up behind him. This had to be Jacob Pearsley, his brother.

"Yes suh." That was all I wanted to say.

"You people don't seem to know the value of things," he grumbled, walked away muttering something else under his breath that I was not able to comprehend.

"Is this one giving trouble?" the other man asked.

"He's doing fine uncle. Luther has been working so hard since he started yesterday," Rebecca said.

"That's their value – to work in the cotton fields and nothing else," replied the feisty old man.

"Let's remember that at all times," Jacob reminded him.

"Dad…uncle," Rebecca protested. I saw Dorothy's face twisted in disgust. I remained calm and pretended that I didn't hear.

"You have a lot to learn," he told Rebecca, "they have cost us too many losses."

"How can you say that Dad?" Rebecca asked, throwing her hands up in the air in disgust.

"Your father speaks the truth," Jacob said.

"I can say anything as far as these…" Mr. Pearsley growled.

Uncle Bob came through the door with a box in his hand. The force in which he came through that door caught Mr. Pearsley off guard. "Their numbers seem to be getting bigger around here nowadays. Where did this one come from?" he asked Rebecca.

"Luther is a good worker Dad. He is only here for a while spending some time with his Uncle Bob."

"Oh! Bob, I didn't know he was family."

"Yes suh, blood of my blood," Uncle Bob said with pride.

"They are all the same," Jacob said, walking away to the other end of the store.

"I thought he could be useful while he is here," Rebecca said.

"Well, Bob is one of the better ones so let us hope Luther will prove himself," he said, walking away toward the counter.

Dorothy's eyes never left the whole scene, and even after Mr. Pearsley departed, she kept looking at the very spot he was standing. Her Grandfather and granduncle must have given her food for thought.

I was right. I walked to Cold Stream at lunchtime to nibble on my cheese sandwich. My appetite had left me following this morning's encounter with Mr. Pearsley himself. The incident had me thinking what it must have been for my father when he lived here, as well as for

Uncle Bob living in Clarkesville all these years. One would have thought things would have changed twenty years later, however, it seemed the situation was getting worse before it got any better.

I threw my sandwich in the water hoping it would attract feeding for any fish that was around. They came with a vengeance. Cold Stream must have been depleted of its feeding habitat. As the sandwich floated on the water, it began to jerk, spin, twist and get smaller.

"Loose your appetite? I couldn't blame you," a familiar voice said.

I was expecting Dorothy. She was there.

"Have your Grandfather and uncle been like that all the time?" I asked, looking around to see if anyone was watching us.

"From as long as I've known them. The older they get you would hope to see some change. Grandfather will never change."

"What have we done to them?"

"Nothing. They just don't like coloreds. Ma and I have spoken with them over and over again. Nothing. Since grandma died a few years ago, Grandfather is filled with anger and resentment."

"Aren't they rich?"

"The richest around here. Anyway, don't take it too hard. You won't see them everyday. They rarely come to the shop…Grandfather is out playing golf with his buddies or at the poker table," Dorothy said, trying to smile to bring a little cheer into the conversation.

"Who are his buddies?" I asked. It was the first question that came to mind.

"Oh! Tim Barker from the drug store, Aaron Riley from the gas station, and Milton Davis, who owns the bakery. There are a few others who play with him from time to time."

"All businessmen eh. Are they as old as he is?" I asked, as if I had no interest in knowing.

"The same age group," she said, coming closer and making me feel uncomfortable.

"I am sure he is having fun then," I said, pretending I was not aware of her closeness.

"I don't mind that because he won't bother us at the store."

"Is Rebecca responsible for the store?"

"Yes. Her brother used to run it. He left for another state, Ma has been doing it ever since." She finished her sandwich and put the bag away.

"For how long has this store been operating? You do get a lot of business here," I asked, uncertain why I was asking all these questions.

"It's been in operation from when Grandpa was a boy. They inherited it from Alfred T. Pearsley. He owned lots of cotton plantations from Alabama to Mississippi."

"I would imagine he owned slaves too," I chuckled in order to avoid the sarcasm that might have been ringing out in my tone of voice.

"You are right. I guess that's why grandpa doesn't like coloreds."

"Like father, like sons," I said.

I could hardly wait to get home that evening. It was my second day at work, yet it appeared as if I had been there for ages.

This morning's incident would always be with me. I had been shunned, ridiculed, cursed and screamed at in the past. However, the tone and language used by Mr. Pearsley, this morning, stung like a bee.

I watched the sun's descent from the window of Uncle Bob's humble abode. I wanted the day to finish quickly. Perhaps a new day would bring a new feeling, a new optimism.

Uncle Bob was lying down in his couch. He was careful not to re-visit this morning's incident at the store. I commended him silently for that. The incident was history; I hoped it remained that way.

There was a knock on the door. "Who is it?" Uncle Bob shouted, unmoving in his comfortable position.

"Benny," came the reply.

I went to the door, turned the lock, gazed into the face of Benny and what must have been his beautiful daughter. She reminded me of Kate.

"You must be Luther," Benny grinned at me. Benny bore the traits of a mature man; there were a few grays sticking out of the side of his head. Faintly visible wrinkles had started to seep through, primarily around his mouth. He was a tall man with teeth as white as chalk.

"This is Maria," he said simply, his voice containing a ring of authority. Benny's daughter was a feast for the eyes. I blushed by just looking at her. Maria had a perfectly shaped face. The calculating stares from those dark eyes were like magnets. About the same height as Lena, Maria was tempting me to compare both of them. I refused to do so – at least not right now.

"Ah! Come right in," Uncle Bob shouted, " make yourself at home."

"I haven't been here for a while and thought this would be a good opportunity to show our faces," Benny grinned.

"You couldn't be more timely," Uncle Bob replied.

"Luther, it is good to meet yuh," Benny said, turning toward me.

"It's a pleasure suh," I said, "glad to meet you, too, Maria."

"It's nice meeting you too Luther. I heard so much about you from Uncle Bob that I'm always imagining what you look like," she said, the dying sun lighting up one side of her face.

"Hmm, that's interesting," I replied, at a loss for words.

"How is it going so far?" Benny asked.

"Some ups and downs, nothing spectacular to speak about," I replied.

"Except your encounter with Mr. Pearsley today," Uncle Bob reminded me.

"What happened?" Maria asked.

"He used some very harsh language to me today. I've since forgotten or trying to forget the incident."

"This is America my friend. The descendants of slaves are still carrying the burden of our forefathers. Take note of every incident you experience here son, and tell your sons and daughters of what we have to go through to fight for our rights and equality," Benny lectured me.

"I'm now seeing a need to do that," I replied, wanting to sound grateful for the suggestion.

"Your father was a lamb, a very kind-hearted man. He was as harmless as a dove. The fate he met was undeserving. Bob and I here tried and we have been getting nowhere because of the secrecy surrounding his execution," Benny said, as all of us took a seat around the table.

"Are you willing to continue?" I asked. I was so anxious to get moving on this, and any thoughts of thinking whether I should have asked, were far from my mind.

Benny examined me closely and so did Maria. They must have been wondering whether this young man was serious about the question.

"Are you serious?" he asked, a thin smile vanishing from his face, "because if you are, I am ready. Maria here is ready, too," he said looking at her.

My eyes twinkled. I looked at Uncle Bob; he seemed in support of that.

"We have a good team here. We don't need more than what we have in this room," Uncle Bob suggested.

"Where do we begin? Your father was a dear friend. We grew to love one another like three brothers here. We owe it to him to prove his innocence," Benny declared.

"My father never stops talking about your father even after all these years. I believe firmly that he wants to get this off his chest. We are here to give a helping hand."

"I feel good about what I'm hearing," Uncle Bob said. "I tried alone, it didn't help. Benny and I tried, and still no breakthrough. It's time to try a team with some younger heads."

"Where, when do we start?" Benny asked, excitement building up in his voice.

"We start tomorrow, the first thing I want to do is to try to find a witness to the alleged crime that my father committed."

"Witness. Yes, we heard there was a witness. That will be a hard nut to crack…we cannot get the information," Benny said.

"Before I came here, I managed to get some information from a library in Canada about lynching. Is there a library around here that we could get some newspaper articles about that crime?"

"There's a library here," Maria said. "I've a good white friend that I could ask to look it up for me."

My heart jumped with the possibility that we could be heading somewhere. "At least, that's a start. We may well hit something there. By the way, did newspapers carry the story?"

"Oh! Yes they had to have, without the shadow of a doubt. It was a big story here among the other folks. Only our community couldn't get the information we need," Benny said.

"If we can locate the witness, we are open to a lot of possibilities. If we can't get the witness, then we'll have to start somewhere else. Who's the oldest man in our community right now?" I asked.

Uncle Bob and Benny exchanged glances. Maria's eyes were on me. "Any particular reason in knowing that?" Maria asked, maybe determining at the same time that she knew the answer. I saw her expression change and suspected she had already answered her question.

"The oldest man would be able to tell us more about the lynching in 1915. Those bloodthirsty people, I am sure, are the same ones that lynched my father."

"You are a smart boy," Benny said. "I have never thought of that.

"The 1915 lynching was a public event. An old timer would know the people responsible," I said.

"You are right," Uncle Bob agreed. "I am thinking that the oldest man…hmm, could that be Titus Carter?"

"Uh-huh, you are right. Dear Ol' Titus must be nearing ninety now. He could tell you about lynching dating back to the 1880's, when they were very commonplace."

"We should pay him a visit on the weekend," Benny suggested.

"I agree," I said. After four days, I was not doing too badly I had to admit.

Uncle Bob fixed tea and biscuits. We sat there talking from one subject to the other. Maria was very talkative; we agreed on a lot of ideas.

"What are you doing Thursday afternoon?" I asked, as they were about to go.

"You are asking my daughter on a date right before my very eyes?" Benny joked.

"Ha! I wasn't even thinking about a date," I said sincerely. "I was more thinking about plotting some strategies to deal with our little assignment here. Remember you said the younger minds could make a difference?"

"You have me there on that one," Benny conceded.

"Well, with that, we can meet at Cold Stream," Maria suggested.

"I can see Cold Stream is a popular place. It's nice and very relaxing I have to admit. However, there's something about it that touches a nerve in me, " I said, nodding my head.

"I can see you've been there," Maria said.

"I spend my lunch time there. Dorothy and I met there today, and yesterday," I said, wanting to elicit some sort of reaction from this beautiful woman. I couldn't help wondering what was going through that lovely head of hers. I began to wonder if I was developing a weakness for women, especially the attractive ones.

"Oh, you're making friends fast, I can see," she said.

"I need friends around here. Without them, I won't reach anywhere. I promised my Grandmother to return soon."

Maria looked at me. She must have been thinking to ask another question. I suspected she must have been wondering whether I was thinking seriously of going back soon?

Somehow, I would have preferred not to answer that one. Right now my mind was bent on returning to Canada. Maybe, I emphasized maybe, Maria had other reasons for believing I could be here for a long, long time.

What would make her think like that? That was the million-dollar question for me. I would pay anything to know if she would take pleasure in answering that question.

Chapter Six

Clarksville was getting more and more interesting each day. I had started to theorize that there was a cloak of secrecy surrounding certain activities in this quiet town. It was not something that had started yesterday, it was not something that would cease to exist tomorrow. This could have started many years ago. One thing was pointedly clear: that cloak still existed today.

The puzzling questions were who and why. My intention was to find out, if I could achieve that, then I would be able to solve the riddle of my father's execution.

It was Wednesday afternoon. I was able to drill out of Dorothy where Mr. Pearsley and his buddies played golf. "What interest is that to you?" she had asked.

I told her I wanted to familiarize myself with the area. She hesitated then said it was Silver Springs Golf Club on the outskirts of town at the lower end of Cold Stream.

That was where I was standing now. To be more precise, I was stooping behind a clump of bushes overlooking the golf course about fifty yards away.

I had to stoop to avoid being seen by Mr. Pearsley, and his friends playing golf.

They were having a grand time. Laughter and winning strokes erupted around the hills bordering the course. Mr. Pearsley and his friends appeared to be in their seventies. Four of them, plus two caddies, were on the field. In the distance, the clubhouse dazzled in the afternoon sun. There were few movements outside the clubhouse although it was too far to see what was happening.

I took a mental picture of the men accompanying Mr. Pearsley. I studied them in every detail. At this moment, I paused to ask myself why I was doing this. Why am I at a golf course watching four rich, powerful men playing golf?

There must be a good reason I convinced myself. I need no further evidence to prove that Mr. Pearsley did not like colored people. My father was accused of stabbing a businessman. These were elderly businessmen who must have been around the time my father was lynched.

This must be a good place to start my investigations. I could be wrong; if there was another way, I did not see that as yet.

I lingered there for another half an hour. I had enough of their playing and laughing. It was time to go.

"You did what!" Uncle Bob screamed. "My goodness! I was here worried about you. What business do you have...playing golf?" he said, lowering his voice.

I had never seen Uncle Bob so angry or upset. I knew he was worried about my whereabouts. Had I told him where I was going, he might have discouraged me. And that was the last thing I wanted on this mission i.e. to be discouraged in any attempts to pursue leads that could help me to prove my father's innocence.

"I wasn't playing golf uncle. Here, take a seat. I want you to listen to me carefully," I said pushing a chair to him. "I haven't been sleeping since I came here uncle. I stare at the stars at nights, relax my thoughts, then examine all the possibilities regarding those who could have been responsible for this horrible murder."

"Hmm," Uncle Bob grunted.

"There's no doubt that the rich people of this town were responsible for this action. One of their colleagues was stabbed, they took it upon themselves to carry out their own vigilante justice. A colored man is of little significance to them, there was nothing to stop them from doing that. Today, the businessmen from that period play golf," I said, getting somewhat dramatic, and taking a swing with my hand in the mode of a golfer.

Uncle Bob was rubbing his forehead while I was speaking.

"You is figuring out something that we haven't been able to do all these years. Son, I think we is onto something here. However, Mr.

Pearsley is not the man in all of this. I think we should rule him out. I don't think he would ever do such a thing," he said, not mincing his words.

"At this stage Uncle Bob, I'm not pointing a finger at anyone in particular. At the same time, I'm not ruling out anyone. Everyone should be treated as a suspect. Surely, our people didn't lynch my father. Where we are starting Uncle, I believe, is the right place."

Uncle Bob twisted his fingers around each other – a sign that he was nervous. Already, I could see he that he was dreading the revelations to come. Me, I was full of excitement that I have something to work on. I wanted to dance, to sing, whistle, shout for joy, although I had a far way to go.

I wished I could tell Grandma and Kate my progress so far. It might be nothing to speak of right now, considering that it was only observations so far. Up to this point, there was no substantial evidence. Deep down in my being, I know I was going to prove this.

"Please take your time and don't go faster than you need to go. The last thing I would want to see happening is for us to accuse the wrong person. Caleb was accused wrongly. We must be on guard not to do the same to other people," he said calmly.

"I agree uncle." I meant it.

On that note, we retired to bed. Before I went off into another world, I summed up Uncle Bob's reaction to my assumptions. His attitude had changed suddenly; it had me dead worried.

I was taken aback to find Maria waiting at Cold Stream during lunchtime, on Thursday. She was sitting opposite my daily seating place on the rock. A basket was in her hand, the odor creeping from the holes in it told me something palatable must be in there. I was right.

"Thought I would carry you lunch," she smiled – a smile that sent shivers down my spine. Maria was truly an attractive girl.

"Thanks. That is nice of you. Is our so-called date on for this afternoon?"

"Of course, I wouldn't give that up for a million dollars. I know that you will soon get tired of cheese sandwich."

"How did you know I eat cheese sandwiches everyday?" I asked curiously.

"Your uncle told me."

"Hmm… checking up on me eh?"

"If you were interested in someone wouldn't you?" Maria said, looking me straight in the eyes. I felt hypnotized, or like a spell had been cast on me. I was startled too that she was so blunt.

"Are you?" I asked trying to sound as if it was news to me. I remember her first visit the other evening and the way her eyes had been glued on me all night.

"I won't deny that. It's not often I have the opportunity of someone walking into my community, impressing me from the first time I set eyes on him," she said, turning away her head as she spoke.

"I can see you are blushing as I am," I chuckled.

"Hmm, at least we have something in common."

"Suppose I tell you I have someone already in my life," I said, knowing that I had taken a big gamble in saying that. I wanted to be honest with her. All my life, I have tried passionately to be an honest man. My Grandmother had taught me that virtue based on her stern belief in the Bible, the Word of God. I had no problem accepting that; I intended to live that way for as long as I had the breath of life.

"Is that person supposedly in Canada?" she asked, watching closely for my reaction.

"She is in Canada," I answered.

"Well, I'm not in any rush. I am willing to wait for as long as it takes," Maria said, smiling confidently.

"Suppose you are going to wait indefinitely, or in vain?" I tried to scare her, just to get a genuine reaction.

"If it's someone I truly admire, I will."

"Hmm, you know what, let's get some food."

Our senses must have told us to leave that dialogue there – for now.

"Oh! You are right…"

We started to eat. Maria brought fresh cornbread, butter, some strips of roast beef, fruits and lemonade.

"Any word from the library?" I asked. I was conscious of someone's presence nearby. I turned around to see Dorothy heading toward us.

"No, not as yet. Er…don't be frightened, I was expecting her any moment," Maria joked.

"I wasn't even thinking about her."

"Now you will," she smiled.

"Hello there, can I join you two?" Dorothy asked, sitting beside us before getting an answer.

"You are already here," I said. "Do you know Maria?"

"I know of her but we have never met," Dorothy said, extending her hand. "It's a pleasure to meet you Maria. Maria is a nice name."

"Oh thank you. It's nice to meet you too. It's such a small town, yet we are complete strangers. It takes someone like Luther to bring us together."

"Isn't that something. There has always been a gulf between our peoples. I wish to God it would disappear at this very moment," Dorothy said regretfully.

"Let's pray it will happen in our lifetime to clear up some of the horrible things that were done in the past," I said.

"The wounds need to be healed. And the healing can only come when we start treating one another as human beings instead of property."

"I agree Dorothy. When the secrets of the past come out in the light, when hatred is shoved aside, we begin to talk to one another, then we are getting somewhere," I replied.

Dorothy paused before answering. I could see she wanted to put thought into her answer. "People such as my Grandfather have built so much hate that only the hand of God can intervene to remove this evil from his heart. I pray for him daily but I see no change. Many times I ask, God where are you in all of this?"

"And yet we know he is there," Maria interjected. "Your Grandfather will have to do his part in order to begin somewhere. He must start looking at us as people, not animals."

"He's getting old and should be making peace with God?" I suggested.

"He inherited it from his father who owned a huge cotton plantation with a lot of slaves. I hate to say this. His wealth came from the backs of your forefathers. He should be grateful to them, although that doesn't sound right. I know, please forgive me. The point I am trying to make is he has no reason to feel that way about colored folks."

My eyes left earth to penetrate the clear blue sky. All I could see was blue. Beyond that, up there somewhere, I know there was a vast universe – stars, planets, moons, galaxies. The evidence of life, the beautiful creation all around were enough to convince me that God existed. And that at one point He sent His only begotten Son, Jesus Christ, to die for the sins of mankind. Yes, for my sins, that of Mr. Pearsley, Jacob and their father.

In my heart, I wanted to forgive them of their evil actions. If they repented before God, I know He would forgive them. That was all right with me because God had forgiven me too. But at this moment I prayed silently to God that although they might have been forgiven that their earthly punishment be given for whichever crimes they were guilty. And not only them, the countless others who were also guilty.

"Is he the only businessman in this town who feels this way?" I asked.

"I hardly think so. Most of the business people in this town may feel the same way."

"That's interesting," I remarked. My hunch was right. Maria should know more than us about the white folks.

We walked back to the store. I had no fear then because it was three of us.

Later that afternoon, Dorothy visited me at least four times. The visits were all unnecessary. All that was on Dorothy's mind was to elicit information from me regarding Maria. On two of her visits she wanted to know if I had talked with Maria often. I reminded her it was only my fifth day in Clarksville.

After work, I walked home with Uncle Bob, planning in my head what I could do with Maria this afternoon. Nothing came to mind. The only thing I could think of was for us to sit and talk somewhere.

Two hours later, Benny brought his daughter over. "I care for her welfare, that I have to bring her myself," he said grinning with me at the door.

"I will take care of her. I will promise you that," I assured him.

Benny came in and we sat around the table like we did yesterday. I assumed it was a kind of mini-conference about our little investigative project.

"I got word to Ol' Titus. He is willing to talk," Benny disclosed.

"Good! Good!" I exclaimed, clenching my fist in conquest.

"There is one thing though," he continued.

"Yes," was all I could say, frightened of the prospect of another hurdle to face.

"Ol' Titus has pneumonia. He needs a few weeks to recover before he can see us. He's asking us to be patient."

"Hmm, I'll wait as long as it takes."

"I'll ask my library friend tomorrow," Maria said.

"Who's she?" I asked. I never thought it was important to ask that question before.

"She is Eva Simms, the daughter of the Librarian, in Clarksville."

"That's a good person to know," I told her.

"She's a good girl, a sympathizer to the plight of our community," she replied.

"You better get out of the house now before I change my mind," Benny teased. I liked him for his sense of humor. Even in serious situations, Benny tried to inject some humor that rendered melancholy helpless.

I reached over, grabbed Maria's hand, and we just sailed out of the house without uttering another word.

We walked up Main Street. From there, I could see we were heading toward Cold Stream. The sun didn't have much light left in it. Soon, darkness would swallow up the whole town. For that reason, we didn't want to venture very far from home.

"Cold Stream again, I presume," Maria said.

"Where else?" I asked. "Cold Stream must be the only recreation area around here. Do you know of any other?"

"How about there?" Maria asked, pointing to a bench beside a monument of the town's founder William Clarke, an Irish businessman.

A concrete figure of Clarke with arms akimbo stretched into the sky on top of a four feet high stone-cut base.

Four benches were around the monument, one for each side. A few yards away, a fountain spurted water above. A few spruce trees enclosed the monument giving some space between the area and Main Street. The setting was a departure from Cold Stream; I had begun to decipher the reason for my sudden attraction to Cold Stream. Something about Cold Stream kept munching at my mind. It had become a part of me in such a short time, furthermore, it was making up for my little stream back home. Maybe that was it, I concluded.

"I'm very much interested in learning more about the Pearsleys. Is there anything you can tell me? I get the impression that Uncle Bob doesn't want to discuss them. He feels obligated to the family, especially Rebecca."

Maria nodded in agreement. "If I tell you something will you promise to keep it to yourself?"

"If you believe I'm going to tell, then don't tell me," I told her.

"I'll take a chance. In other words, I think you are able to keep your mouth shut."

"That's a start."

"I know your uncle is reluctant to pursue what we're attempting to do now," Maria said.

"You mean finding the people responsible for my father's death?

"Eh huh. I don't know why he's so hesitant to pursue the matter."

"It's simple. They are putting bread on his table. I guess mine too," I admitted. "Rebecca is a nice woman and although her father is a pig, I can't help but feel some obligation too."

"I wouldn't want you to defeat your purpose here if push come to shove," she suggested.

"Not at all."

"Let us move onto something else. Tell me about your lady friend in Canada," she said softly.

What could I say? I couldn't deny that something was growing between Lena and myself. "Lena is about my age, a very nice girl who will go to the ends of the earth for me. She is waiting for my return."

71

"Hmm, I'm about your age. You shouldn't be more than twenty-five. As I said before, I'm willing to wait for as long as it takes," she smiled.

"I can see you are a determined woman."

"I prefer if you say confident young woman," she shrugged her shoulders.

"Whatever you say. Where are the young men around here?" I had never thought about that before.

"Some have moved, some died in the war, the few remaining are already taken. I guess I must have missed my match," she giggled.

"You are younger than ever. There's ample time to find a mate."

"The right mate I dare say," she said, an earlier smile vanishing from her face.

"Tell me what you know about Mr. Pearsley?"

Maria's eyes rolled in her head. The fading light might have concealed that, if I hadn't noticed it closely.

"I know more about Mr. Barker. I thought you would be more interested in him."

"Who's he again?" I asked, trying to put a face to the name.

"Tim Barker owns Tim's Drug Store right over there," she pointed to a huge white building between two trees beside the monument. "He is as influential as Mr. Pearsley."

"Is he the bald and stocky one?" I asked, an image of his beefy face entering my mind.

"I thought you didn't know him."

"I saw him on the golf course with Mr. Pearsley

"He is as sly as a fox. His past is tainted with blood," she said scornfully.

"What do you mean?" my curiosity simmering to a new high.

'He was a hero in the World War. He returned home wounded to a hero's welcome. As a result, he could do nothing wrong. Some of us believe he has ties with the KKK..."

"Ku Klux Klan, I have heard of them," My hands began to sweat at the mention of that name. I pictured cross burning, some poor, innocent, colored man dangling from a tree in the pitch black of the night, with the light from their torches shining in his face and obscuring his view.

"Anything he does no one dare to question it because of his fame. I believe he ceased that opportunity to do a lot of wrongs – even lynching."

"Lynching! You mean he could have something to do with my father?"

"I'm not saying that. I honestly don't know. Until we have some solid evidence we can do nothing. If you should talk to some white folks they will tell you that Mr. Barker is an angel sent from God. I really don't know what to think," she said.

"Hmm. Suppose we get some evidence he was involved?"

"We go to the State Attorney in Jackson. "

I was learning more each day. I guess a hot headed young man like me whose sole aim is to prove the innocence of my father have no clue how he will go about doing that, once the evidence is there. Initially, I thought about going to a big newspaper with the story hoping they would publish it. That alone, I thought, would be enough to re-open the case.

Now, I was hearing the way right here. Indeed, there is a way to prove it through the court, once I have enough evidence to get the prosecutor's interest. I just never thought about that before. I had been too busy trying to find the culprits.

"Well what else do you know about Mr. Barker?"

"He is a strange man living in a strange world. I know some colored folks he gave drugs to when they were sick. I really don't know... How could he be a KKK and helping us?"

"How do you know all of that?"

"My friend Eva Simms. She is the same one who will be getting the information from the library. Mr. Barker is her uncle and she speaks well about him."

"Something just doesn't add up at all. This Barker is a kind of mystery."

"Honestly, I believe he's part of the problem. He gets on some people's nerves. He doesn't like Eva keeping company with me...segregation, he believes in that firmly."

"Is it truly in existence in this town?" I asked. I had a keen interest in this subject and want to be more knowledgeable about it.

"You better believe that. This is Mississippi, the heart of cotton country. Cotton and slavery could be described as the same thing. One cannot exist without the other. I couldn't go to a white school. Today, the children…innocent children are still separated," Maria said, a tone of anger in her voice. "Some of our laws make segregation legal; until they are changed there's nothing we can do about it. We can't even vote."

"I must commend you for your intelligence. You speak very well. What's your life's ambition may I ask?"

"My ambition is to be a Professor of History, and to marry a nice young man…" she said, watching me from the corner of her eyes. "What's your life's ambition?"

"To clear my father's name…after that I will think about it. I like the soil, so maybe I will become a big farmer."

"Pursue your dreams my dear because that's what keeps us going."

"You sound like a musician," I said. I have been noticing the way she curled her lips to answer my questions in such and calm and relaxing manner.

"I do sing, and I write songs too. Next time we meet I will bring my guitar," she smiled widely.

"I look forward to that. Bring it to church, on Sunday," I suggested.

"That's a good idea. I will most certainly do that."

A loud, crashing noise shattered our conversation, as splinters of glass showered around us, some even attempting to stick into the lower part of my leg. I could feel the tingling sensation as fragments of broken glass tried to make their way through my trousers.

Maria grabbed my arm, clinging on to me in fright. I grabbed her arm in return, making the space we occupy much smaller. It was almost dark now, and we could not see anything. All we could tell was that a bottle might have been thrown, crashing only a couple feet away from us. Bottles didn't flow out of mid-air; they had to be thrown by someone or something.

I listened for footsteps. There was none. I listened for any sound that could have given me a clue on what was going on. Again, there wasn't anything I could glean.

By now, both of us were flat on the ground, our knees scraping on the pavement. A streak of light from a building shone on the monument, although it was not enough to reveal what had happened, or if anyone was around.

We waited in the same position for about three minutes. All was quiet. A few businesses remained open. I raised my head and tried to look around the area near me. There was no one near to us. I whispered to Maria that we better go. We did that without even thinking about it, should any danger be lurking by.

On my way home, Maria held my arm with a clutch of fear. She was frightened. She had good reasons to be, seeing nothing like that had ever happened to her before. I walked Maria to her house, cautioning not to mention anything about the incident to her father. Maybe the incident had nothing to do with us – a mere accident. Well, I was hoping it was that simple. Before I left, Maria kissed me on the cheek – the first time I had ever received such a gesture.

The snores of Uncle Bob filled the room by the time I reached home. It was about eight thirty. With nothing else to do, going to bed was the only logical thing.

I must have been lying there for about an hour, twisting and turning. I know I wouldn't wake Uncle Bob whose snores suggested he must be in deep sleep.

My mind recalled the events of the day – the lunchtime meeting with Dorothy and Maria, the addition of Tim Barker to my investigative list, and the bottle-throwing incident. A lot of things had happened in such a short time.

I could see now the need to speak with Titus. He could give us a more solid lead. If Eva came up with something from the library, that too would be an added boost. The identity of that mysterious witness would even be better. I wanted the precious opportunity to ask why the silence after all these years.

Chapter Seven

Rebecca handed me some money after work, on Friday, while I was sitting on a bench at the back of the premises. I was so indebted to her that I didn't bother to count it. Besides, it was the first time receiving payment from someone for work done.

"You did a good job this week Luther. There will be much more for you in the coming weeks," Rebecca smiled, a gust of wind parting her hair, pushing it into her face. She brushed the hair away from her face waiting for my reaction.

I could see why Uncle Bob spoke highly of this woman. She was rather attractive. No wonder, Dorothy had some of those characteristics. Was he that captivated by her looks that he preferred not to discuss her?

"Thank you ma'am. That's very kind of you. I need the help more than you need mine," I laughed.

"C'mon Luther please don't speak like that. We are all here to help one another. Oh! I didn't get to speak to you since that incident with my father. For my sake, can you please ignore him?"

I couldn't say no to the person who handed me my pay a minute ago. It was no surprise Uncle Bob was behaving that way. I saw the reasons now, unless he had other motives.

"He is getting old and senile and sometimes I have to ignore what he says, and forgive him for some of the venom that comes out of his mouth," she said sincerely.

"I have forgotten that already ma'am. Nowadays, I try to focus on the things that are meaningful in my life," I replied.

"That is a smart thing to do Luther," she smiled thinly.

"My time is limited. And I have to spend it wisely while I'm here. I don't have time to waste."

"I'm proud of you Luther. Keep it up and you will succeed in whatever you do," Rebecca advised me.

"Thank you ma'am," I said, nodding in agreement.

Uncle Bob told me he would be coming later so I should go ahead if I like. I was about to leave the back door when Dorothy came up to me.

"I was wondering what you are up to over the weekend," she said.

"Me…well, I will go to church, relax…"

"And maybe visit Cold Stream…" she said, finishing the sentence.

"No, no, I don't have that on my agenda," I said hastily.

"How about Maria?" she asked.

"Maybe I'll see her in church," I replied calmly, trying not to show surprise by her question.,

"We could go for a walk, if you don't mind," she quipped.

"Dorothy you know that's a big chance around here. It's not that I don't want to go…it could be dangerous. Inter-racial relationships aren't lawful here. Have you forgotten that?" I reminded her, somewhat annoyed by her disregard for my safety.

"Marriage. We're not married, we are only testing the waters. Don't you feel some sort of excitement to try? I do. Maybe we can change things here," she giggled.

"I'm not willing to take that chance. It will be many years before any changes. I don't want to end up at the end of a rope."

"No, no, no. That's all in the past," she replied with a frown.

Perhaps it was a mistake to answer the way I did. Dorothy was the kind of individual to seize on opportunity to make her point. "Maybe we can plan that walk for some other time," I suggested, realizing once again that I could have answered much more appropriately than that.

"I will hold you to that," she teased.

We said goodbye. On my way home, I could beat myself for my dismal performance with Dorothy. I must have fallen under the same spell as Uncle Bob. I should have rejected her altogether.

Uncle Bob did not come home until some minutes after ten. He found me sitting around the table reading the book of Psalms.

"I thought you would be asleep by now," he said, putting down a brown plastic bag in front of me. The smell sent a message that there were some baked products in there.

"I'm not going to work tomorrow. This is the right time to catch upon some reading."

"Good son, that's good. Do you want a piece of apple pie? Did you fix something to eat?"

"I'm alright. I'm not hungry." That paper bag was not from a store or bakery, it would carry a label if that had been the case. Rebecca must have baked that apple pie. I don't think it would be proper to ask him where he got it. It was none of my business, furthermore, he was the owner of the roof over my head.

I guess the big risk in asking such a question was that I could have been drawing false assumptions. On the other hand, so what if Rebecca gave him an apple pie. He did admit going over there for dinner most Sundays.

"I expect you to take anything you want here son. It's for both of us," he said, joining me around the table.

"I got paid this afternoon. I don't know how much I should pay you for staying here," I said.

Uncle Bob coughed at that moment. "Pay me? What on earth are you talking about son?" he asked, staring at me. "Son, do you know how much of a pleasure it is to have my dear brother's son right here with me, eh…do you know how much? Money ain't gonna pay that cost because it is worth much more than money."

"I don't know what to say," that was all I could mumble.

"I failed in finding your father's killers. The least I can do is to put you up for as long as you want. You were in Canada with my mother all these years and to think of it, I should be the one paying you," he shrugged.

"Thank you uncle. But she's my mother as well as my Grandmother; she has been taking care of us all these years," I stated proudly.

"Son, you save that money and whenever you go back take it with you to help out the situation back there. I am getting old. I am getting enough to get by. Don't need no mo'e my son."

"Thanks again Uncle Bob."

A flash of lightning peeped through my parted window, as the fresh morning air forced itself into our room waking me in the process. Within seconds, thunder rolled in the heavens, then the rains came with a pounding noise on the roof of our small house.

I feared Uncle Bob's humble house would buckle under the powerful raindrops that were battering the roof. Half an hour later, the rain finally stopped; a noticeable calm came over the town on this very wet Sunday morning.

I had ruled out church today, however, that was to change when the golden rays of the sun found their way through trees, cracks and crevices, shining directly into the room. I jumped out of bed and turned around to nudge Uncle Bob to get out of his slumber. Uncle Bob was up already; the smell of coffee told me so.

"What a good start to the day," he called from the kitchen. I walked in to find him frying eggs.

"It's a good day to go to church and to praise Jesus, our only hope," I said.

"Yeah son, sure sounds good to me. In the past, my father use to tell me the stories about our Grandfather how they had to get up early in the morning, rain or shine, to go into those fields. If it wasn't to pick cotton alone, it was also to plant tobacco or corn. The rainy season was time to plant, yes sir, a time to plant and a time to reap. Come reaping time they had to endure the chilly mornings as well as the very hot ones."

"That was awful. I don't know how they survived those grueling days," I said, with resentment.

"We have a lot to be thankful for. We must praise God for this son," he said, pulling out a chair to begin eating.

Church was crowded as usual. The hope for us colored folks was in Jesus Christ. Only He alone could get us out of our misery. It was no wonder then that they flocked to church like this.

Maria was among those attending with her guitar. After service, we found ourselves a nice comfortable seat under a tree at the back of the church.

"Are you ready to hear me croak?" she laughed.

"Whatever is uttered from your mouth I am ready for it," I said.

"Remember now that I am the songwriter and composer," she cautioned me.

"I will," I replied.

The guitar opened with a melodic introduction. Her fingers were all over the fret of the guitar running up and down the strings. She was no stranger to this instrument.

Upon the white clouds I see
A new hope for all humanity
Despite the horrors of our past
We know our redemption is coming fast

O what a wonderful story to tell
That God has delivered us from the claws of hell
Sing praise, sing praise for evermore
Tell it to everyone from shore to shore

I look and there were no tear or fear
Only joy, laughter, happiness and cheer
O death where is going to be your sting
When to our God we will be a priest or king

O what a wonderful story to tell
That God has delivered us from the claws of hell
Sing praise, sing praise for evermore
Tell it to everyone from shore to shore
Tell it to everyone from shore to shore
Oh yes, tell to everyone from shore to shore.

I couldn't wait to start clapping, as it didn't take an expert to recognize talent.

"I can't believe you wrote that," I said. "Did you truly write and compose that?"

"Of course I did," she reassured me.

"That's talent. What are you doing about it?" I asked seriously.

"Singing for Jesus I suppose until I can get into some other things with it."

"Are you worried about what happened the other evening?" I asked.

"You know what? I haven't even been thinking about it."

"I'm trying to get it out of my mind. I can't...it keeps coming back. Who could have done such a thing?"

"There are several possibilities," she said, clutching her guitar.

"How about sharing them with me?" I asked, anxious to hear the possibilities.

"I don't see a problem with that. If we have enemies both of us should know about them. I have narrowed it down to two people," Maria said, putting down the guitar.

"Yes."

"Tim Barker or Mr. Pearsley."

Those were the only two names I could think about. Yet I had a tough time convincing myself that it could be either of them. "Those are old men," I shrugged.

"They don't do their dirty work. It is always someone else doing it," she said, looking around the room.

"Any names?"

"Yes. Be on the lookout for the most muscular man in Clarksville. You can't mistake him for anyone else, because Joe Tucker behaves likes he owns the town. He's loud, sloppy, and likes to be seen and heard. He has the backing of these powerful men. He does what he pleases."

I met Joe the following afternoon. After a slow and lousy Monday, Dorothy and I were closing the store. Uncle Bob and Rebecca went on an errand.

Joe measured me from top to bottom and from bottom to top. His eyes were as cold as a cobra. I almost closed the door on him because we were fifteen minutes past closing time. He fumed, turned pink, and clenched his fist in a rage that only Dorothy could have calmed him down.

"Does that dirt know who am I?" he demanded to know from Dorothy, "…you give them an inch and they take a mile. Boy, when you see a white man coming into this store…this store, you open the door for them, and don't stand in their way. Do you get that boy?" he snarled.

I remained silent. Dorothy tried to intervene; he almost shoved her away. Joe's mind set was on me. From what I had been observing, he wanted to whip me as if we were living in the 1820's.

"I am talking to you boy," he snapped.

To remain silent is golden. I always remember that from Grandma. Now, I am applying that principle and stand ready to face the consequences.

"This is a store Mr. Tucker, not a boxing ring. Luther was only doing his duty. We are long passed closing hours y'know," Dorothy said, moving closer to me. She was frightened. I could see that, wishing I had the wherewithal to alleviate her fears. I wanted to say something badly. Instead, I bit my lips.

"Answer me boy!" Joe yelled, observing my mouth.

I stood my ground.

"You don't understand English, or do you speak some weird African language," Jacob Pearsley said, as he came in

I pretended Jacob was not there. He was furious. By this time, Joe had given up his attempts and allowed Jacob to take over.

"This is insubordination. Rebecca! What's someone like this doing in this store?" he demanded to know.

"Luther prefers not to say anything, Uncle. Despite what you may think he and Bob work so hard around here. We are grateful for them."

"We will see," Jacob said.

"I would advise you to leave Mr. Tucker," Dorothy said calmly.

Joe whirled, turned, then stormed toward the door. "We will meet again; this time it will be different," I heard him cursing under his breath.

Jacob picked up a newspaper, and then left.

"Where did he come from?" I asked Dorothy, referring to Joe.

Dorothy's face lightened up now. She was at ease and she started to smile.

"I could see you were troubled," she said in a teasing way.

"I have to admit I was worried for you," I confessed.

"Thanks for being that concerned," she replied.

"You know I am beginning to care about you," she said, coming up behind me as I closed the front door. She edged so close I could smell her perfume.

"That's nice but…"

I couldn't go any further with that statement. Dorothy put her hand around my waist and squeezed me from behind. I was startled out of my mind much more than when Mighty Joe was present. "You know this is trouble…" I mumbled, trying to remove her hand off the grip she had on me.

"No one can see us now," she said.

"Suppose someone comes in right now," I said, turning around to face her.

"That won't happen because I already locked the back door," she assured me.

"Dorothy! Are you out of your mind?" I said with rage. Think about me too! I am the one who's gonna get in trouble, not you. I still can get lynched!" I protested.

The word lynched must have struck a chord somewhere because it was the last word I had said, and the sound of it was hanging in mid air – in silence.

Dorothy made one step backward, released her grip on me, and stared at me blankly. She placed her hand on her mouth as if she was holding back a scream. Something was wrong, and I had every intention of finding out.

"Is something wrong Dorothy? Well…something is wrong, yes…I can see that."

"W-What do you know about lynching?" she stammered.

How could I answer that without raising any suspicion? I wondered.

Uncle Bob might have told them I was the son of another brother, and not the one that was lynched. So far, my father had not been discussed since my arrival. For now, I hoped it would stay at that.

"Any colored person alive in America should know what lynching is about!" I answered, hoping that was a fair statement.

"Are you that fearful?" she asked, walking away from me.

"I cannot rule out anything. It's not a matter of whether you are innocent or guilty, you know that. It's a matter of whether you are a colored, or a victim of circumstance."

"You don't have to be colored because some white people have been lynched and people from other groups," she corrected me.

"You can't deny that the majority has been colored," I said, moving away from the door and hoping she would follow me. I wanted to get out of this scene desperately because should the situation present itself again, there was no guarantee what could happen.

Dorothy followed me toward the door leading out of the store. I was relieved. Nevertheless, she was not ready to go home; she wanted to chat or spend some time with me. Maybe she wanted to keep me away from Maria this evening, although we might not even see each other. She stopped before we could step out into the evening sun.

Normally, after work we go our separate ways. Her house was not far from the store whereas Uncle Bob's was further away. My encounter with "Mighty" Joe could have changed our departure habits this afternoon.

"What are you doing later?" she asked.

As she asked the question, another one popped up in my mind adding to my dilemma. Suppose Mighty Joe, as I was now calling him, was waiting for me outside, or on the way home?

"I don't even know at this stage. I am confused and tired," I said with a yawn.

"Something interesting is happening tonight that you, as a colored person, should be aware of for as long as you are here," Dorothy said calmly.

"What is it?" I asked searchingly, my eyes moving all over her face.

"I cannot tell you. I want you to see it with your very own eyes," she challenged me.

"This must be important. It sounds very important," I admitted.

"It is…for your survival, justice, freedom and liberty," she shrugged.

"What are you talking about?" I demanded, wondering whether she was enticing me to go along with her wherever she was going. I couldn't help. I was already interested with all this justice and freedom stuff. Those words appealed to me very much nowadays.

"As I said Luther, I want you to see it with your own eyes. When you do, you will be able to have a better understanding about Clarksville."

"Hmm, I have no choice now. You have made me become so curious that I cannot refuse. What do I have to do to go with you?"

"Give me a kiss on the cheek," she suggested.

"You know that's not a good idea," I said, making a step backward to communicate disapproval with that.

"I won't set a foot out of here until you do that," Dorothy said commandingly, making no attempt to move from where she was standing.

I didn't know what to do. She did. Dorothy made a step backward inside the store to accommodate her demand. I made no move so she made it instead. She came right up to me and kissed me on my forehead.

"See, it's not so difficult after all," she grinned like a mischievous child.

"Hmm, we better go," I said, trying to conceal my discomfort with her impulsive action.

"At 9 o'clock, meet me at Cold Stream," she informed me.

"Cold Stream…I thought we were going…"

"We are only meeting there. In other words, the journey begins at Cold Stream," she smiled again, obviously feeling triumphant that she got her wish.

"Does your mother know you are going?"

"Of course not!" she replied with a frown. "She will be fast asleep by then. Can you get out of your house at that time?"

"Uncle Bob will be asleep too."

It was nearly nine o'clock and Uncle Bob should have been asleep by now. He was going off, not fully sound asleep as yet. That was where I wanted him to be; I would have to leave when I was certain he would not awaken easily.

The palms of my hands were wet with sweat. My heart was racing faster; soon I could be getting a tension headache. Undoubtedly, I was nervous about what I was getting into. I had to; Dorothy was so vague about her invitation it could be regarded as something that was next to blackmail. Of course, this would depend on the outcome of this invitation.

I waited patiently for Uncle Bob's snore. I stood by the window eyeing the huge full moon slicing through the clouds on the horizon to make its presence known to the blackened heavens. A silvery glow illuminated every crook and cranny of the night sky. It would be a beautiful night.

I waited five more minutes before I got the signal. The clock was saying ten minutes after nine. I made my way hurriedly down to Cold Stream, walking on a back road that was behind the buildings on Main Street. I didn't want any light on my face tonight.

At Cold Stream, Dorothy was sitting calmly on my daily seat when I got there. She stared in my direction when she saw me approaching in the moonlight.

"Come, follow me," she said calmly.

I followed like a puppy trailing its mother. We passed over a footbridge on the lower end of Cold Stream and headed south along the shores of the stream. The reflection from the moonlight on the water gave us enough light to help us decide whether to place our feet on rocks or in water.

"We mustn't make any noise. If you have to speak, please whisper," she reminded me as we walked along.

Funny, I thought. I was at her disposal now. She could easily make her demands...maybe get them as well. I hoped to God that would never happen. She was walking close to me, holding my hands at times. She was so near that I could smell the freshness of an earlier bath.

We walked for about half an hour. By this time we were far, far away in the woods, away from the flickering lights of Clarksville. However, before us I could see lights or a light twinkling in the distance ahead. She slowed down.

"I don't want to frighten you," Dorothy whispered, "we are on dangerous territory as you will see. We must be quiet. We cannot hang around for along."

The time was imminent for me to solve this riddle once and for all. Throughout the trip here, all I could think about was what I was getting into with Dorothy. It was difficult not to convince me that she was not up to something sinister, something far away from my mind or intention. So far, so good, if ever there was any merit in this adventure, or soul-searching trip that was as dubious as its leader.

As we drew nearer, the lights grew brighter. As the lights got brighter, the voices became louder. I had my first allusion there. My body shook with chills not from the temperature of the night; it was from what I feared was up ahead. If this trip could help me solve the mystery of my father's death, then it would have been essential. On the contrary, if it had nothing to do with it, I believe it would instill in me a sense of purpose, a better understanding of human behavior, as well as the notion that evil was the exact opposite of good.

Dorothy squeezed my hand, clasping it into hers in an attempt to have a firm grip on me, should I decide to take my feet in my hands. That was the only conclusion I could draw from that move. Maybe I was wrong. She drew me to her and kissed me quickly on my lips.

I was dazed although not for long, given the circumstances unfolding before my eyes. This was one smart girl who knew how to take advantage of a situation when it suited her. My mind was not on her kiss at all. I was more concerned with the spectacle unfolding before me.

"Please forgive me for bringing you here. If you are hurt and offended, please forgive me. I thought you should see this so you can know the people you are dealing with…believe it or not, it is for your protection. Tell no one, not even Uncle Bob."

By this time we were curled up behind a rock overlooking a ledge where we could clearly see what was happening below. The lights shone feebly in our faces adding to the fear that was building up in me. For the first time in my life, I felt real cold fear.

I had heard stories about what I was seeing. I had been told stories, too, read stories when I did get an occasional newspaper from Lena. Poor Lena, I thought. If she ever saw me now what would she think? I was in the company of a white woman alone in the woods. So far, nothing serious or compromising had happened, except for that innocuous smack on the lips moments ago. Could I ever convince her of that? Dorothy had done something I would have a long time forgetting. Sooner or later, I knew I would have to tell Lena what I was seeing tonight. I will have to tell my Grandmother and Kate too. What my eyes were seeing and my ears were hearing were a once in a lifetime opportunity.

"Tonight white brothers, we welcome Jordan Coombs as the newest member of the Ku Klux Klan." There was a salute from the speaker. Incidentally, the voice sounded familiar to me. It was too much to concentrate on the speaker, as I felt bewitched by the burning torches, a huge cross that was on fire, and the twenty or so masked figures wearing all white.

Their white apparel struck a striking contrast against the blackness of the night. Where they stood, trees were all around; the lunar glow was not touching that part of the earth, adding to the already hideous and taunting atmosphere.

So here I was only a few yards away from a Ku Klux Klan's initiation ceremony. Was this a dream or a fairy tale? The Klan, which was formed after the Civil War, was becoming a force to be reckoned with, especially in the Deep South. They hated colored people, and would never apologize for saying that. They were for segregation, and somehow, I believe they had their roles in lynching too.

Dorothy was as silent as the grave. With her hand over her mouth, she observed the proceedings calmly. At times, she watched the expression on my face. I suspect she must have wondered what was on my mind.

"Do you recognize the speaker?" she whispered.

I kept looking behind me in the event they had spies around scouting the surroundings. "No," I answered.

"Listen closely," she advised me.

"These mud people are taking over this country. We cannot allow that to happen to white people," the speaker declared, "we have to rise up one day soon and drive them back to the jungles of Africa, where they belong."

"I cannot believe it," I whispered.

"Who?"

"Joe."

"You could be right. He could be the Grand Marshall of the Klan. That is why he has so much talk around town."

"Do you know anyone else in that group?"

"I don't, unless they speak."

The thought of the Pearsleys ran in my mind. Are they here tonight? I would want to ask Dorothy that. I could only hope that if they were here tonight, one of them would be speaking. Given my experiences here, so far, the possibility of that was not at all improbable.

Chapter Eight

The moon was nearly half way in the star-lit sky. Down below, the camaraderie was still going on. For little less than an hour, I remained in my crouched position; my feet were numb.

Dorothy was becoming restless so I knew it would soon be time to go. We had decided to wait a while longer, should the other speakers join Joe in revealing their identities, unbeknownst to them.

Dorothy was probably recovering from shock after she had identified the voice of Clarksville's most popular local politician – Mayor Rudolph Bangor. She had placed her hand on her mouth in fright.

"Should we go now?" she whispered.

"Whenever you are ready, I am," I whispered back, looking below as the hooded racists were down to some serious deliberations. We could hear the rumbling of voices, but were unable to decipher what was transpiring. It would be much easier to hear if a speaker was addressing the gathering.

"I don't know how much more shock I can deal with tonight. Mayor Bangor is enough."

"It would be very interesting to see some of those faces behind those hoods. They look so intimidating," I said, speaking normally as I tried to lower my voice.

"It's getting late. I think we should better go."

"Okay. I never dream of seeing something like this," I replied in a higher tone, forgetting for a few seconds that I was in enemy territory.

"Shhhh. Tell me on the way," she said, with a finger on her lip. She grabbed my hand and we cautiously made our way down from the small embankment we were sitting on. I must have stepped on a dry branch or something of the sort. All I know, there was a loud cracking sound that disturbed the deathly silence of the night. Any kind of suspicious sound would draw their attention.

A horse neighed somewhere in the thicket beside us. I doubted whether that was related to the sound. I heard two shouts coming from the direction of the gathering. My eyes turned around in my head as I looked in that direction. Dorothy stared at me in the dark - she nodded her head in the direction that we came from. The signal was to run.

Before I started to accelerate beyond my normal pace, my eyes caught a torch coming through the trees. There was another, then another; the numbers grew to maybe about eight. I had expected to hear automobile engines roaring to go, but apparently, horses were used to reach this remote part of the forest.

I jerked Dorothy's hand to indicate that we had to move faster. She was not looking behind as I had been doing. The voices told us that indeed they were coming. We had to move fast – very fast.

"There! There! Two of them!" one man shouted. The torches were much nearer, if they were able to see the two of us in the dark.

"Don't let them get away!" I heard another man yelled.

We ran as fast as we could. Dorothy chose to follow the same trail that we came on. She must have traveled it before, as we didn't have any difficulty finding it. Our feet searched in the dark for the right spots; we found them alright. That enabled us to move much faster.

Dorothy's breathing was getting heavier. It would be a matter of time before we would have to stop. Me, I was fine for the time being having enough stamina to hold out for as long as we could.

I glanced behind me again. This time I didn't like what I saw. The men were gaining ground; the light was getting bigger and brighter. The voices were getting much louder.

"There they are! Keep moving boys!"

If they kept on closing the distance between us, they would eventually catch up. It was only a matter of time. I had to think of a strategy. Up ahead, the river narrowed a bit; that meant the water should not be so deep. Back home in Canada, I often go for a swim during the summer in my favorite stream but only during the day. Tonight, I would have to swim in this stream; I didn't have an option unless Dorothy could not swim.

"Can… you swim?" I asked softly.

"Yes, I can."

"We have to swim across at that dark spot…now! They won't be able to see us unless they are near."

"Let us go for it," she said willingly.

We ran a few more feet. The lights were coming around a bend in the distance, the glare reflecting across the rippled surface of the water. Now was the chance. Thank God! The water was not really cold. We drifted away from the shore in the shadows of the trees, until we could not stand anymore. The water swept us off our feet with the current moving us along the direction we wanted to go. Both of us did sidestroke to abate noise, and to minimize disturbances on the surface.

By the time we reached the other side, the lights were almost upon us. Immediately, we jumped behind some foliage watching as the running lights moved up along the shore on the other side.

The men ran along merrily. Their speed was not that fast. They ran up to the spot where we had changed our course and stopped right there. They might have been too tired to go around that huge bend.

"We lost them," I heard someone said. We were facing them almost directly from the other side of the river.

"Unless they stop somewhere."

"Should we take a look around?" someone asked.

We held our ground. They could see us from where we were. If they decided to come across like we did, they would come right into us.

Dorothy cuddled up beside me. Her wet clothes produced shivers. My instinct informed me - cautiously, I tried to keep her warm by putting my arms around her. A low and faint feeling, too, was overwhelming me.

The men couldn't decide whether to resume their chase or to return to their camp. An argument developed; there were disagreements as well as agreements. A consensus about whether to continue the pursuit had eluded them. I noticed one man who walked away was heading back to camp. Three others followed then the rest of them gave in. It was easy to detect their movements when the moonlight shone directly on their white robes; they glowed brightly along the shore.

Dorothy breathed a sigh of relief, I managed to do that too. We lay there for a while with our backs on grass and gravel. We were too tired to talk, too tired to think about anything else, too wet for comfort. All we wanted to do was to get home.

Home came an hour later after we walked arms in arms for the entire journey. Both of us needed to support each other physically. We felt like injured soldiers coming in from the battlefield.

I walked Dorothy to her doorstep. It must have been around midnight or later than that. She squeezed my hand, thanked me and quietly opened her door. Then she kissed me goodnight.

My journey home was quick. Every step I made I looked behind me, anticipating seeing someone following. Uncle Bob was still snoring by the time I climbed into bed. Good. Tonight was one night after all – certainly the memories would take me to the grave.

The sun woke me the next morning. The rays squeezed through my window uninvitingly taking up residence on my pillow. Uncle Bob was already gone. To my surprise, the sun was high in the sky.

I jumped to my feet; they couldn't carry me. I was forced to lie down in the bed. A very painful cough sent spasms throughout my body while my chest felt as if a dagger had been lodged in it. My eyes hurt whenever I tried to turn them. When I coughed again the pain was worse than before.

I was sick, very sick. I must have used up all my strength last night; now I felt robbed of all my energy. I wanted to sleep again. Fortunately, my warm bed was already waiting.

Footsteps in the house woke me some time during the day. I had expected to see the sun shining through my window the moment my eyes opened again. There were no rays from the sun; in fact the sun was shining on the other side of the house because it was mid afternoon.

"Are you awake?" Uncle Bob called from the kitchen. "I have some nice, hot chicken soup here for you."

I tried to speak, however, it was very painful for me. I limped out of bed and made some feeble steps into the kitchen.

"What happened to yuh las' night son?" Uncle Bob asked.

I was about to answer to admit our secret trek to the camp of the Ku Klux Klan.

"You were coughing for most of the night," he added. "This morning when I got up you were still coughing. You told me you don't think you could make it to work because you were sick."

"I told you that?" I asked.

"You don't remember?"

"No, I think I was having a bad fever that could have made me say anything."

"Rebecca sent some chicken soup for you. It is good," he grinned.

"That was timely."

"Dorothy is sick too. She went home to cook it for her then came back to work."

"Who took care of the store?" I asked out of concern.

"A.T. Pearsley. He was raving mad. He kept asking how come you and Dorothy were sick at the same time with the same sickness?"

My heart pounded against my chest. I truly felt sick. What on earth was going on here? How could Mr. Pearsley link the two of us to having a common ailment? What was the meaning or motive behind such a suspicion? My hunch was right last night.

In my sick state, I recalled that at one point last night I examined the possibility of the Pearsleys standing proudly in one of those white robes. I based that suspicion only on his reaction toward me the first time we met.

For him to wonder about our sickness, the Pearsley's must have been there last night. I would imagine that the men who chased us went back and report to the entire camp that they lost us. He could have deduced that we escaped by swimming across the river. Getting wet could have triggered whatever was ailing us.

Two people were spying on them last night. The Pearsley's were aware of that. Today he had to help out his daughter at his store after two employees contracted a very bad cold or flu at the same time. Did the rather cool waters of the river have anything to do with that? At least one of the Pearsley's suspected that. Dorothy didn't say how she knew about the meeting. To think of it, she could have heard from either of them in some conversation. I didn't know how to ask her about that.

"Sickness is sickness, how can he question that?"

"You know him. He's a heartless man."

"Did Rebecca say how Dorothy is doing?" I asked. I felt guilty for being responsible for her illness.

"She's not doing well. She has it very badly…roasted with a fever all morning," Uncle Bob said, looking at me rather strangely.

"I can't afford to rest uncle. I have to get to work." My throat was not that sore anymore, after I assumed Mr. Pearsley was getting suspicious.

"Rebecca says to take as much time as you need," he replied, still watching me closely. Uncle Bob wanted to ask me something; I could see that. However, either he didn't have the guts to do that, or he was not concerned.

"I don't mean that type of work. I mean to prove my father's innocence."

"Oh that…Maria came by the store today too. She will be coming over to look for you. She whispered to me that she has some good news."

"Good news about what?" I asked, as I started to sip my chicken soup. It smelled and tasted very good.

"Her friend Eva found something from the newspaper," Uncle Bob said, taking his eyes off me now.

"That is very good…" I was delighted to hear that. I had no complaint to make regarding our investigation so far. One by one, things were falling into place. What was next?

Maria was the best person to answer that question. About five o'clock, she answered the question while she was reading the story about my father's lynching. It was taken from The Clarksville Chronicle and dated May 20, 1926. The headline read *"Criminal Lynched in Clarksville."*

According to the story, Caleb Nesbeth was lynched for stabbing a store-owner in broad daylight. An eyewitness, who chose to remain anonymous, was quoted as saying he saw my father standing over the wounded man. He was subsequently arrested. During his first night, an angry mob stormed the jail and lynched him.

The story ended by alleging that members of the Ku Klux Klan might have been involved in the lynching.

There was silence in the room. I looked from Benny to Uncle Bob.

"Are you both aware of the presence of the Klan in this town?" I asked them.

"We know they are around. What we don't know is how active they are," Benny answered.

"I tend to believe that story that they could have been involved in the lynching. I know that I need proof but that will come in due time."

"Maybe Ol' Titus can answer that," Uncle Bob suggested.

I had forgotten about Titus. "Oh, when can he see us?"

"I don't know. He is very sick and will need some time to heal," Benny said.

"What do we do in the meantime?" Maria asked.

"That is a good question," I answered. "Now that I'll be away from work for a few days, I will rock my brain to see what I can come up with. We have to find out who is this witness," I said, relishing in the hope that we will eventually get to that witness.

"And if he is alive or living in Clarksville," Maria said.

"Can your friend help?"

"She would be willing to help. That means I may have to fill her in on what we are doing. The question is: how much do we want to divulge at this stage?"

"Let me think about this," I said quickly.

My head was feeling light. Something was happening to me. I could not explain it. Everyone in the room became a blur; their voices were fading away. I was sweating profusely feeling like I was going to faint. That was the last thing I remembered.

I woke up in a daze. I didn't know what day it was, or what time of day. I remembered that one morning my eyes opened for about five minutes. Someone had given me something to drink. I descended into a strange world of dreams and hallucinations.

My father came to me crying and pleading for him to be taken out of bondage. He said he could no longer live under the shadow of a criminal. How could they do this to him, he begged to know, when in fact he had never killed in his life? He was even afraid to hunt because of his fear for hurting someone.

Grandma was there too. Her face was a mess, as she couldn't stop crying. Proving her son's innocence, she said, was tantamount to winning a million dollars. As for Kate, her face was in her hands all the time. She was trying to reach out to my father who was sliding away from us. Lena came screaming on top of her voice. She was angry about something I didn't understand. She stayed far away from me.

I tried to reach out to Lena but it was futile. There was something, maybe a barrier or an invisible force preventing us from holding hands. I, too, started to shout. At that point, l came out of my dreamland the second time. Someone was standing over me. At first, I could not recognize the person. Then an outline of Maria's familiar figure began to gradually form in my mind.

"Hi," I said, finding it a challenge to say another word.

"Hi. How are you feeling?" Maria replied.

"I don't know. I am too weak," I mumbled feebly.

"You will be for some time. That is what the doctor says," Maria informed me, getting a little closer to the bed.

"Doctor…he was here?"

"He came twice."

"Where I was all this time?" I asked, barely moving my lips.

"You were right here…burning with a fever that couldn't break."

"I must have been saying all kinds of things," I said, remembering Kate had a very high fever at one time and was speaking incomprehensible things. My mind remained on them in Canada. I hope they were okay.

"You did. God was with you. The doctor said you could have died."

I offered a silent prayer of thanksgiving to the Eternal. I became very concerned about Dorothy.

"Did Uncle Bob say how Dorothy was doing?" I asked, watching her reaction.

"She has it badly, too, but not as bad as you. She is doing fine."

I knew some things must be running through Maria's head, wondering like Mr. Pearsley, how come the two of us were felled by the same illness.

"A very bad fever bug must have flown through this town," I said, deliberately hoping it would ease some fears.

"I hope it ain't coming my way," she grinned.

"Uncle Bob is okay?"

"He is sure fine. He went to work," she replied with a smile.

"I don't know how to thank you," I said, holding her hand. "How long now I have been like this? What day is today?"

"Today is Saturday," Maria said, squeezing my hand.

"Do you mean I have been like this since Tuesday night? My goodness, I can't believe it!" I blurted out, trying to get up out of the bed.

"No, you stay right there. You ain't going no further. I have been placed here as your guard," she teased.

We talked a little longer then off I went to sleep again, fearful that I would once again be faced with those haunting dreams.

On Monday morning, I was ready to go again. I got up early, stretched my muscles then ran around the house. The warming rays of the morning sun brought a renewed vigor to my body.

"I can see you are sure ready to go," Uncle Bob said, watching me from the doorway.

"I am, that bed isn't for me anymore," I said, breathing very hard.

"Rebecca will be glad to see you. She asked about you everyday," he said, watching for my reaction.

"Certainly not A.T. Pearsley though, or Jacob."

"Oh! Forget about them," he shrugged, dismissing the thought with a flash of his hand.

"Dorothy is the one concerned about you. She was at work on Saturday. Ever so often she came to ask me to come and check upon you."

"She wanted to come to visit. I know that...around here such a thing isn't a good idea. Colored folks may visit white folks...not the other way around," I said, getting accustomed to the fact that Uncle Bob didn't like to talk about that subject.

"You're so right son. What can we do? It's the system we have been living with since slavery."

"We have to fight the system, Uncle. Somehow, somewhere, we have to get the power and the clout to do it. Already, there are groups fighting for our civil rights for the last fifty or so years. Progress is slow. We have to be patience."

"Well spoken son, but now it's time for work."

Yes, I would go back to work for Rebecca and her racist father. Yes, I would continue to work for as long as I could, then I would expose all the guilty ones for their horrendous crimes against humanity. I would also expose those deep hateful faces that were hidden behind those white, profane hoods for what they were.

Dorothy and Rebecca were truly happy to see me back at work. I knew Dorothy wanted to give me a hug; she dared not to do so with her mother standing right there.

No one mentioned anything about the two of us being sick at the same time, much to my relief. There was a lot to do in the store. I wasted no time getting down to some serious work.

Lunchtime crept on us stealthily. I skipped out of the store longing to see Cold Stream, grateful for the thoughts of comfort it gave to me on my mission to prove a point. Cold Stream was there all right. Today, it appeared more beautiful and serene than ever. The water just flowed with ease; the trickle was loud enough to notice.

No one was in the park. My guess was that Dorothy would have been there by now, however, she was nowhere in sight. She could have changed her mind.

I had my lunch after I felt as if I had hadn't eaten anything in days. My trousers had more than the usual amount of room, indicating the few days without food, had robbed me of a few pounds. The sandwich dissolved in my mouth making me feel for another one. There was none, so I would have to be satisfied for the time being.

I went back to work to find Dorothy slumped behind the counter, with her eyes swollen. They were as red as a cherry. She had been crying for a while, it seemed. All kinds of possibilities raced through my mind. No one else was around to my great relief.

"What is wrong?" I asked her.

She remained silent.

"Did I do something wrong?" I asked timidly.

Dorothy nodded; tears were building up in her eyes again. She turned her head away from me. I got the message. Somehow I was convinced I was the problem. I wanted to know why.

"We musn't talk to each other again. We can only speak if it has something to do with the store," she sobbed.

"What are you talking about? Who decided that?" I demanded to know.

"My Grandfather," she said softly, her voice trembling at the mentioning of his name.

Mr. Pearsley again. Hmm, something sinister is going on, I told myself. This Grandfather is up to something that I cannot place a hand on or fathom out at this moment.

"Why, may I ask?"

"He says I'm white and you are a Negro. He says you have your place in society, I have mine. We're completely different, he insists. My Grandfather has threatened to take me out of his will if I ever develop a friendship with you…you know what I mean," she said. "He says it is the law of the state."

"How convenient," I said, quite peeved.

"I think it's something more than that," Dorothy admitted.

"And what would that be?"

"I better not say right now until I am positive about it."

Dorothy must have been thinking like me that her Grandfather was at that Klan rally. He thought the two of us were the people spying on them. Hence his decision to restrict our friendship.

"I know what you are thinking," I said, watching her closely.

"What?" her eyes blared out at me.

100

"I prefer to remain silent for now."

"Can you please tell me? I ain't going to get no sleep tonight if you don't." Dorothy wasn't crying anymore.

"I can't, I don't want to cause any bad blood between us. I'm making an assumption that could be utterly ridiculous," I emphasized.

"I promise to take it as calm as possible. You have nothing to fear. Nothing surprises me anymore."

"You promise?"

"I do."

"Okay. Are you thinking your Grandfather or uncle was at that Klan rally the other night?" I asked, searching for the right words in order not to sound too judgmental.

There was silence…and more silence. Dorothy head's fell from its upright position and bowed over the table. She did not answer or even look at me. She could be crying again. It was difficult to determine that.

"Can you please leave me alone?" she mumbled under her breath.

"I will."

Dorothy's promise meant nothing. That was telling me that my suggestion to her didn't go over well, as I must have hit something close to home.

I did the work I was being paid for. I went home with Uncle Bob, armed with bewilderment about the day's turn of events with Dorothy. Maria came over to see how I had been doing; we chatted for a while. I decided to walk her home because there were some things that I wanted to get off my mind.

"Is there anything you can tell me about the Pearsley's that I need to know. I must have asked you already. However, they are getting more and more interesting to me?" I asked as we came near to her house.

"Has something happened lately?"

"As a matter of fact, yes. Today, he told Dorothy to make sure she only has a working relationship with me. If she didn't she would be left out of his will."

"That was pretty harsh. Hmm, what did her mamma said about that? He doesn't like us, we know that, should that come as a surprise?"

"I suspect it is something more than that."

"Well, you know a lot. Pour it out on me dear."

"I made one suggestion to Dorothy today. She got really mad with me. I haven't been able to get a word out of her since. I hope what I'll tell you won't bring the same results," I said, noticing that it would soon be very dark.

"If you think it will make a difference then don't tell me anything," Maria insisted.

"I'll take a chance. I don't believe you would keep malice with me."

"Okay brother then shoot," she replied, a smirk came then disappeared in seconds.

"I believe one of, or maybe the two, Pearsley's support the Klan..."

"You what? Say that again, I need to hear it once more."

Maria's reaction was vague. I didn't know whether to interpret that as something good or bad. I repeated the statement.

Maria turned around to face me. At the same time, she extended her hand. "Welcome...please join the hundreds of brothers and sisters around here who feel the same way as you do."

I took her hand and squeezed it. "For a moment I didn't know what to think. Now I do. Tell me though, why are so many people quiet about it? That's a horrible thing to do."

"Once again, the Pearsley's own the town. They employ some of our people, they put bread on our tables."

"And might even be guilty of crimes against those same people," I fumed, not at her, rather at the hundreds who live everyday with sealed lips, or indifference to the horrors and injustice meted out to them.

"None of them can be trusted. You cannot rule out anything regarding them. Tell me, what made you think that way?" Maria asked, leveling her stare at me.

"This is the other part of the story...the difficult path," I emphasized.

"I am listening."

"Last week Dorothy told me she wanted me to witness something with my own eyes. Hmm, I was curious. I followed her along the river to a camp of the Ku Klux Klan."

"What! Are you kidding me?" she asked, raising her voice to a pitch I never heard before.

"No I ain't," I almost yelled at her. I wanted to get over telling her this. I wished to say everything all in one breath.

"You ain't kidding me?"

"No. We were spotted shortly before we were about to leave. We had to run for our lives. If we didn't swim across to the other side of the river, we would have been caught. We were dead tired," I explained, remembering in vivid details, my attempt to outsmart the racist throng on our heels.

"That's why both of you were sick at the same time."

"I guess so. Jacob has been watching us closely since he started asking why the two of us were sick at the same time. My conclusion was that he was among those hooded men at the camp."

"Did she recognize anyone else?"

"Yes. Joe Tucker…Mayor Bangor."

Maria was so stunned she had to lean against a post nearby.

My entrance into Clarksville had started to raise some questions. Even the most powerful man in the town had started to wonder about me. Maybe I was finally onto something, or was it the other way around, something was onto to me. I found that out while on my way home.

Chapter Nine

The huge figure standing in the pathway was not hard to recognize in the shadow of nightfall. The dim lights from some nearby buildings cast a silhouette over him, making it easier to figure out his corpulent physique. It was Mighty Joe Tucker. I believe I knew what he wanted.

The moon was already in the sky. Nevertheless, the night was dark. He must have chosen that spot directly because light from a nearby building, maybe a factory, shone directly in the path leading off Main Street, joining Maple Street.

Joe was grinning at me mischievously with outstretched arms, beckoning that he had me conquered with nowhere to run. That might have been so, unless I decided to reverse and run like a scared rabbit. I couldn't though as I was very curious to find out what Joe had up his sleeve.

"Hey boy, we don't want you mud people hanging around our beautiful white girls," he said, his face becoming a shadow in the faint light. "If I were you, I would be gone from this town in a heartbeat. We don't want any more of your kind in this town, you get what I mean. Where did you come from anyway?" he asked.

My weapon of silence I decided to use again.

"If you don't answer me I'm going to break your bones," he snapped.

I braced myself for harm. I kept watching his hands and feet, monitoring his every move. If this mean looking Joe was going to charge like a raging bull, then I must be ready for a stampede.

"Answer me boy! Answer me or else…" He stopped to place his feet across to cover the entire width of the pathway. There was no space for me to pass by. Joe meant business, serious business.

"Are you deaf mud boy, are you a mute? A mute cannot work in a store…you want your job back, then answer me?"

Joe waited for about a minute for my answer. When he didn't get one, he made a step toward me sending his muscular hand into my face. I didn't read that move to be a blow coming. Even with that notion, I was not about to remain stationary in my position to find out. All I had to do was lean my head slightly to the left. That I did, and poor old Joe, the invincible one, found himself off balance. His might could not help now; he was headed for some stones along the pathway. To add frolic to his awkwardness, I nudged him in the side. One of Joe's feet levitated a bit and all of his two hundred and forty pounds went sprawling on the rocky surface. I heard flesh and clothes rubbing against gravel.

Joe cursed under his breath. The moment he regained his balance he was back on his feet with the agility of a monkey. He was maniacal and who wouldn't expect him to be.

"You black…I will get you for this…" he snarled. Joe charged once more. Had I allowed myself to be intimidated by his words, his huge fist would have already been bruising the tender flesh on the side of my face. I had no plans to make that happen. Therefore, when Joe made a wide and powerful swing to my right, I repeated my earlier performance, this time coming completely out of his angry path, by barely leaning over to the left.

Joe saw it coming, only that it was too late for him to do anything about it. The might and virility of Joe sent him tumbling on all fours. He remained in that position for a few seconds, although all kinds of swear words came off his vocal chords.

"You will rot in hell! I will get you for this…you will pay for this boy," he said biting his lip in the dark.

I was in the opposite position from which I was coming. The place where I was standing before the encounter that was where Joe was lying now cursing and swearing incessantly.

I walked away from the scene, leaving Joe to figure out his next move. At home, Uncle Bob could not understand how I could get Joe on the ground without a real fight.

"I am glad you whip him son. However, there will be consequences to deal with. Watch your back at all times… be prepared," he advised, with some humor.

"I've been doing that since I came here uncle. I think we are onto something, there's no giving up now," I said.

"What else have you found out?"

I had been entertaining some very disturbing thoughts about Uncle Bob's attitude in my quest to find out more about my father's death. I theorized that he expected the information to be delivered on a silver platter. Uncle Bob did not want to rock the boat, whereas I was more than willing as long as it could get me somewhere. My Grandma, Kate and Lena were waiting on me. I was in Clarksville, nearly a month now, with little intention of being here much longer.

"I only have some ideas to work on – nothing concrete. As soon as I'm onto something I will let you know. I want to ask you something uncle."

"Go on son."

"Have you ever told Rebecca and Dorothy that Caleb was my father?"

Uncle Bob smiled. "A long time ago, I told them Caleb had a son. The second day you came Rebecca asked me if you were that son."

"And…"

"I got my thoughts together quickly son. I remember that discussion we had at the house about trying to find the people responsible in a secret way. I said to myself I ain't going say nothing to Rebecca about this, I told her your father lives in the east. They believe you are from the east."

"Benny and Maria know everything though?"

"Yes, they do because they is in this together with us," he grinned.

"Good uncle. I thank you for that."

We went to bed after that. I did not feel triumphant over the defeat of Joe. On the contrary, I had a disturbing feeling that this was only the beginning of war.

I went to work as usual doing what I had been asked to do. Dorothy paid me no attention; I did not get even a salutation. That was all right with me seeing that I was on borrowed time in Clarksville. My interest now was to do what I had to do and get out.

I had decided not to go to Cold Stream today. I joined Uncle Bob at the back of the store where we nibbled on our cornbread and butter. We ate mostly in silence returning to our jobs afterwards.

Come time to go home, I was the first to try to retrieve my bag. Uncle Bob trailed me to reach it. However, someone else was standing by the hanger in the back where my little lunch bag was kept. A.T. Pearsley had my bag in his hand.

Uncle Bob walked up to my side, after he saw I was going no further. No one said anything. Dorothy came into the room followed by her mother.

Mr. Pearsley threw the bag at my feet. I heard a sound coming from the bag that I had never heard before. In the afternoons, I usually take home an empty bag. This afternoon, it seemed, someone else packed my bag for me.

"I could have you thrown in jail for this," Mr. Pearsley declared.

"For what?" I asked.

"You don't know that stealing is an offence boy," he growled.

I bend down and picked up the bag. It had two tins of beans in it and a bottle of soda pop.

"If I chose to take you down to the Sheriff's Office, you would be arrested right away. If it was back in the days of old, you could be lynched," he said.

Just like my father, I said to myself. "You know I didn't do it."

"How could you!" Dorothy screamed at me. "My mamma rescued you by giving you a job now you turn around and steal from us. How could you do such a horrible thing?" she cried.

"I didn't do this," I repeated. Uncle Bob looked at me in silence. I would have paid a million dollars to know what he was thinking. Rebecca said nothing.

"You expect us to believe that?" Mr. Pearsley asked, making a semi circle around me. His walking stick tapped on the floor reminiscent of powerful raindrops beating down on a thin roof.

"How can I prove my innocence other than to tell you that I didn't do this?" I said, feeling my eyes getting watery with shame creeping upon me. My Grandmother grew me up well. She always reminded Kate and I never to take what did not belong to us. That was a cardinal rule along with one additional one: 'speak the truth always.'

"Around here the word of a colored person cannot stand against the word of a white man. Are you calling me a liar boy?"

It would be detrimental to offer a comment, or an answer to that question. My best bet would be to let that one go.

"You don't deserve to work here," Dorothy said. "You better go now."

I looked at the two women and the two men in the room. I got the message – even from my uncle. I rushed through the door running as fast as I could until I reached home. I rushed in my room, got my things together and started to pack my bag. My sole intention was to get out of Clarksville as soon as possible. I could think of nothing else.

The events of the past week had been weighing too much on me. I had thought mistakenly that I was getting onto something regarding the death of my father. Now I had to try to save my own skin. Joe did not hit me physically; the hit came in a different way. Skillfully, he had planted, or arranged to plant those things in my bag.

At that very moment, it dawned on me that there was more to it than that. What was Mr. Pearsley doing at the store at that hour? How did he know about it? And the million-dollar question was; did Mr. Pearsley have anything to do with my unpleasant meeting with Joe?

I dropped my bag immediately. Where did I plan to go at this time when things were falling into place? I sat around the table to think for a while. Half an hour must have passed before I realized that Uncle Bob was not home yet. What was taking him so long? Did he believe that story from Mr. Pearsley that I stole goods from the store? I was troubled – deeply troubled.

Fifteen minutes later, the door opened; Uncle Bob walked in followed by Maria and Benny. Maria came over to me right away.

"I am sorry for what happened," she said, holding my hand. "We know you didn't do this. Where do you think you are going?" she asked, looking at my bag on the floor.

"Son, you ain't gonna pull out on us now eh?" Uncle Bob interjected, speaking for the first time since I was accused falsely this afternoon. "We know they all planned this to get you to stop working at the store."

I was relieved to hear that. Uncle Bob was caught between two fires. He wanted to keep the job he had been struggling with all these years. It was in his best interest not to have said anything.

"For a moment I was bent on going. However, it dawned on me now since I'm too far into my mission now to go, I won't be pressured by a bunch of racist members of the Ku Klux Klan."

"KKK…what are you talking about? Uncle Bob asked.

"They are…I saw them," I disclosed.

"Saw them? What are you talking about?" Benny asked. He was curious with a determination to uncover the truth about these powerful and influential people.

"Remember how Dorothy and I got sick the other day. We went up the river to the meeting place of the Klan."

Uncle Bob was not so pleased to hear that neither was he displeased. Benny waited to hear more. Maria was hearing a familiar story.

"They saw us when we were leaving and they chased us. Dorothy identified Joe as well as the mayor. We ran as fast as we could. The only way we could have lost them was to swim across to the other side of the river. We must have picked up something that is why we got sick at the same time."

"Do you mean you saw the KKK with your very own eyes?" Benny asked.

"I did."

"Son, to many of our folks, the Klan could be a fairy tale. You had an opportunity many have not had all these years."

"The only person I couldn't identify is Mr. Pearsley. He could have been there. I have reason to believe that now. I'm going to prove it somehow, one way or the other."

"Dorothy believe you stole those items," Uncle Bob said.

"I cannot help that. I will prove my innocence before I leave this town," I told them convincingly.

"Where do we go from here?" Maria asked.

"Give me a day or two to decide," I suggested.

Next morning, I woke up with a nagging headache. Uncle Bob had left for work. I was alone in the house with no work to do. I had plenty of time on my hand, in fact, too much time.

It was time to check out Clarksville. With no work to go to, now could be my opportunity to shorten whatever time I had left in this town.

I stepped out into the bright morning sunlight. The warm rays burned my cheeks. It felt really good. I looked above at the clear blue sky, except for the fleecy looking clouds creeping up from behind the mountains to the east of Clarksville.

I took about five minutes to reach the center of Main Street. The street was busy with automobiles and people. They were all white folks. As a matter of fact, I was the only colored person right now. I had no choice but to be conscious of that given of my experiences over the past two weeks.

My feet carried me without any direction. In other words, I was walking to nowhere. As I came to the end of the street, the human and vehicular traffic was getting scanty. I preferred that. Cold Stream was on the other end of the street. All I had to do was to make a sixty-degree turn in order to get there. I didn't rule out that right now, however, the store beside had a sign that said "B&P Drug Store."

Initially, I could not figure out the reason for B&P. Of course, it means Barker and Pearsley; Tim Barker and Jacob or A.T. Pearsley. That was rather cute.

Should I? I asked myself. What business would I have in there anyway? I thought of something I could buy for Kate, Lena and grandma. Would a drug store be the appropriate place for that? I could only find out by going inside.

I pushed the narrow glass door timidly. It gave way to my exertion and invited me in. I stepped in quietly, hardly wanting to be noticed. A girl, with her back turned to me, was in the far corner of the store looking at some products. At first glance, I thought it was Dorothy, however, I ruled that out because she would be busy at the store now. If the two people speaking at the counter had seen me, I certainly would have been of interest to those two pairs of eyes. Joe and Tim were involved in a deep conversation.

Suddenly, I made a U-turn deciding in a split second that here was not the ideal place to be at this time. The door slammed behind me before I could reach it. I hated that moment. There was good reason for that because both men turned to see me heading back through the door.

"Hey boy," Joe called out to me.

"Who is that?" Tim Barker asked loud enough for me to hear.

"The same one," I heard Joe whispered back to him.

"Who said you could come in here?" Joe demanded.

"Let him come in," Tim said.

"You want this type around here? I have a score to settle with him and I want him in the street right now. Lend me your whip," Joe said.

"Whip? What are you talking about?" Tim asked with a frown. "You cannot do that. Hey boy, you stay right where you are."

Joe moved towards me. No one else was in the store to bail me out, there was no place to run except through that door. Thus, I was beginning to believe my goose was cooked.

Joe had a wide, wicked, grin on his face. He scratched his unruly beard while he moved closer. By this time, Tim was coming from behind the counter to join Joe.

I was preparing for the worst. That was all I could do right now. I blamed myself for what was about to happen to me. If a lion is in your pathway, Grandma would remind me, take another route.

"Jacob and A.T. allowed you to go, I won't…"Joe growled. "You are going down to the jailhouse with me right now boy," Joe said,grinding his teeth.

"What are you talking about?" Tim asked, coming around the counter and standing before me.

"You didn't see him…trying to steal from your store? Even if you didn't, pretend it has happened…" Joe told a bewildered Tim Barker. Surprise was painted all over Tim's face, as much as it had covered mine.

Tim was dumbstruck. I was shaking like a leaf. The thought of jailhouse and what happened to my father sent shivers down my already sweaty spine. Dear God, what am I going to do? I prayed silently. My eyes went for the door; my entire body was about to follow suit. It was too late.

Joe reached out toward me, his heavy hand slapped me against the side of my head. Undoubtedly, he must have put all his weight behind it. For a moment, I thought I was outdoors and it was night. The stars I saw flashing in front of me disappeared quickly. Then there was blackness.

I could feel the sensation of crawling out of sub consciousness. The first object that caught my eyes was the iron bar. Where I was lying had a hard surface - a bed without mattress. A sharp pain struck me at the side of my head; everything started coming back to me…the drug store, Joe's grinning tobacco-stained teeth, and his fleshy hand coming at me.

He must have either dragged or carried me down here. I had become fully conscious now with the voices I heard coming from the front of the jail.

"I was there! He didn't do nothing." The voice was that of a woman. It sounded familiar; I was confused, hence my inability to recognize the voice.

"I'll have to take your word on it ma'am."

I heard footsteps coming toward me. My eyes were glued to the floor watching for the first steps that would emerge from around the corner. The sheriff's heavy boots pounded the wooden floor, followed by a much lighter footstep that sounded like a light tap on a door.

I could see their outline the closer they came in my direction. My eyes moved up from the floor to the two figures that emerged at the door of the cell. Dorothy stood there beside the sheriff. To say I was shocked would not have been an exaggeration. What was she doing here?

I thought I would have seen an angry face; one like the day we last spoke. That was not so. Dorothy was not smiling neither was she crying.

She seemed concerned – very concerned. There was no other reason to explain her presence here now.

"You better be grateful to this young woman. She's your witness. If her family were not a well-respected one in this town, I wouldn't be letting you go. I don't want to hear of anymore trouble from you here boy," a burly-looking Sheriff Tom Thorton said, the moment he turned the key in the door.

I was not certain what I should say. I was embarrassed to say the least.

"Thank you ma'am," was all I could say in that awkward moment.

Dorothy didn't answer me. "Thank you sheriff."

Outside the front of the stonewalled building, Dorothy chose to answer me. "It was the first time you called me ma'am. I hope it will be the last."

"Hmm. I thought I saw you in that store."

"Of course I was there. I saw you come in and tried to avoid you seeing me. After I heard Joe's accusations, I knew trouble was coming," she smiled at me for the first time since she came to my cell.

"You were the last person I expected to come forward."

"I know. I don't blame you for that because of what happened back at the store."

"You still believe I stole from your store?"

"No. I know now that it was a set up. My Grandfather, uncle, and that snake Joe are all guilty of that. I'm getting to despise him so much. I'm sorry Luther…truly sorry."

"We all make mistakes," I muttered under my breath.

"My mistake might have cost you a job," Dorothy said, turning away her head from me.

"How?"

"I should have spoken up. I should have known that you would never have done such a horrible thing. What will you do now?"

"I don't know. It is so difficult getting a job around here…when you are colored," I said. " I may very well go home,' I said, playing wise.

"Perhaps you can work around the house," she said, biting her lips.

I could see she didn't like the idea for me to leave. "I don't have much choice now. How's your mamma doing?"

"She's not doing so okay. She keeps getting these headaches. That's why I was at the drug store to get some painkillers."

"Does she believe I stole those things too?" I wanted very much to know that.

"Not for one moment. She keeps telling me you would never have done such a thing. She wanted to say something…couldn't find the guts to do that. She keeps blaming herself for not speaking out in your favor."

"I know it must have been difficult for her."

"Anyway, I have to go now. Come to the house tomorrow morning before we leave. We'll see what can be done around there."

"Is your mamma okay with this?" I asked hesitantly.

"We were talking about it last night. I don't think there will be a problem."

"What about your Grandfather and uncle?"

"They don't have to know anything. They hardly come to our house anyway. They prefer to play golf and poker with their friends."

"We'll see," I said, wondering if I would actually turn up at the house tomorrow.

I left Dorothy on Main Street, using a side street to take me to the small burial ground where my father and a few other colored folks were buried. It was so quiet. There was an uneasy silence in the atmosphere. I stooped over the grave so I could remove some weeds and other vegetation that had started to grow on it. I kept talking to myself like my father would hear what I had to say. My assurances were that his killers would be brought to justice. I must have been there for about two hours before I decided to leave.

From the burial ground, I went to Cold Stream. Everything was there as usual, its presence making me feel a little homesick. My predicament over the past twenty-four hours had altered my concept of the surroundings. I was coming to the conclusion that Clarksville now had several demons for me to deal with. I had started to consider seriously what was really wrong with this town.

My favorite seating place gave me comfort for exploring some inner feelings. The park was almost empty except for an elderly couple sitting on a bench near the entrance. I felt alone. That solitude sent me into a world of exploration and meditation with my mind focused on the trickling water.

Clarksville seems to be one complex town, ruled by one family while everyone else seemingly conspires to ensure that it stays that way. It is a den for racist KKK members. The poor colored folks live under the tyranny and threat of this group. Even the sheriff is under the control of the family; Dorothy had spoken and Sheriff Thorton jumped to her command and released me.

My father sacrificed his life because of this conspiracy. No one was willing to speak up even though they knew he was innocent. How would I be able to prove that? That was my headache.

I started to devise a plan in my head. Beginning as early as tomorrow, I would begin to execute that plan. The first place to begin would be at Rebecca's house. Information was what I needed and maybe that would be the best place to find it.

I lingered around Cold Stream for another two hours; totally captivated by its charm and overwhelmed by its beauty. I was about to leave when Uncle Bob came rushing to see me.

"Dorothy told me what happened," he said breathlessly. "What the heck is going on around here son?" he blurted out in anger.

"I wish I knew. You know what uncle, the problem is always here and only surfaces when someone is a threat. I may be seen as a threat but I couldn't tell you how."

Uncle Bob scratched his beard while thinking about what I had said. "You may be right son. They don't know who you are. That is a puzzle though. Why would you be seen as a threat?"

"I've witnessed the Klan in action. That's a good reason."

"Huh, I agree. That's when it becomes dangerous."

"We're moving along and although information is getting scarce that's no reason to stop?" I assured him.

"I wonder about that sometimes."

"Do you mean you have doubts about where all this is leading?" I wanted to ask Uncle Bob that question long ago. Now was the opportune time.

"I have to admit that I'm tempted sometimes to tell you to quit by returning to Canada," he said staring at the stream.

"I couldn't deny that I don't get those feelings too. Uncle Bob, I have to keep telling myself that the only reason I'm here is to prove my father's innocence. That I'll do, no matter what the cost. Already, I lost a job and today I was thrown in jail. If that didn't stop me, nothing else will, only death."

Uncle Bob made no comment. I guessed he concluded that nothing would change my mind.

An uneventful week went by in Clarksville. It rained most of the time. I could not get to do any work around Rebecca's house although I doubted there was a lot to do there. My feeling was Rebecca and Dorothy just wanted to make up to me because I had lost the job at the store.

I stayed indoors most of the time thinking about back home and how much longer I would be here for. From all appearances, I could be here for a while as long as all the pieces of the puzzle were taking some time to come together.

Maria came by the house Friday evening. I had not seen her since last Sunday at church. She planted a kiss on my cheeks. That was no surprise; I sensed she wanted to do that from Sunday after I had told her about losing the job. Maria wanted to comfort me. I was grateful to her for that, as I truly needed some kind of encouragement. Everything had happened so quickly.

"Hmm, you are in a romantic mood this evening," I told her.

"I'm always like that when it comes to you…you should know that," she said teasingly.

"I must be too busy with the thoughts that are occupying my mind."

"You are right. I hope this thing is over soon so we can have some time to talk…to spend more time together," Maria suggested.

"Any news on the front?"

"I haven't been able to see my friend Eva. She must be busy."

"What about Titus?" I said, almost forgetting about him.

"He should be well soon."

"Oh! if I could only find that witness."

"That's the key," Maria said, reaching out for my hand. "We'll find that witness."

"Who could be so cruel and heartless not to speak up?"

"It doesn't take much. If a person hates you it's not very difficult to do something to hurt you. That is what the Klan does."

"Are you saying they could have been involved?" I asked, simply because I had been examining that possibility, too.

"I don't know…maybe not, maybe."

"I suppose Dorothy is on speaking terms with you again," Maria asked.

"She has been very nice to me. I cannot deny that."

Maria didn't like that. It was easy for me to figure that out. "Be careful with her. She cannot be trusted. I know what she did at the jail was a good thing. Apart from that, keep four eyes on her, know what I mean," she smiled, dropping a hint that I picked up. In other words, she was cautioning me about getting close to her.

"There's something I must tell you though you'll have to see me through on this. You'll also have to be patient. It's a part of plan I have in mind."

"I am listening," she said attentively. Maria was the kind of woman who could listen to a lengthy conversation without interrupting. She had that attribute that didn't take me long to find out.

"Dorothy and Rebecca don't know I'm Caleb's son. They think I'm from the east, the son of another brother living out there. Now, I am convinced Dorothy has information that could help us. I want to open up a little to her. I don't know how far I could go though."

"Are you positive about doing this?"

"Last week, we were talking," I said, remembering how she wanted to kiss me, " the word lynching came up. She was frightened to hear me say that. From that I concluded Dorothy knows something about what goes on around here."

"What would you tell her?"

"I would ask her what she knows about lynching, if and when the right opportunity comes along.

Maria straightened up in her chair. "That's a good way of approaching it. As I said earlier, she cannot be trusted. Furthermore, you cannot allow her to suspect anything."

"You're getting me nervous now. You see Uncle Bob told me he didn't say anything to them. Suppose he doesn't remember saying that to them? I would be in hot water. I get worried about that."

"Uncle Bob loses his memory sometimes, that is a concern we cannot overlook," she cautioned.

"I was thinking of suggesting to her that I was fearful that I could have been lynched while in jail. Do you think she could draw any conclusions from that?"

"We couldn't rule that out."

"What do you suggest then?"

"Hmm. I'm thinking," she said, poking a finger into my neck.

"I want to ask you this. How much longer do you intend to stay here? It must be difficult for you with your family all the way in Canada."

"It's difficult. I cannot deny that. Maria as long as it takes, I will be here," I said. She would be pleased with that answer considering that deep behind those charming and penetrating eyes was an intention to get closer to me. Maria would strike, so to speak, at the right and appropriate time. To think about that possibility now might be premature. If, and when, that situation presented itself, I would deal with it, I reminded myself.

"It's good to hear you say that. You know what I mean. You have been here such a short time, yet I'm already thinking you have been here all along. There's a void to fill, as far as my life is concerned. Luther you are filling it. Please don't say anything right now," she smiled.

What could I say anyway? "You are flattering me now."

Maria came closer and gave me a hug.

118

Chapter Ten

I presented myself at Rebecca's rather stately house on Monday morning, some time before nine o'clock. Georgian architecture was evident all around. My first thought question was whether slave labor was involved. I reached in time to see them about to leave for the store. They were both glad to see me.

"It's good you could come. Thank you for that, because it means a lot to me," Rebecca said, coming down the steps to meet me. Dorothy followed behind her.

"Make yourself at home. I'll show you around before we leave," Dorothy said.

"Thank you both for giving me this opportunity…again," I said.

"Don't mention it, you are an intelligent young man and deserve every chance you can get," Rebecca replied.

"Thank you ma'am."

"We have to get going. Dorothy will show you around," Rebecca said, walking away.

The first place that Dorothy took me was an abandoned cotton mill in the far corner of the backyard. Cobweb was all over it although it seemed to be providing the right environment for crab grass. I wondered why it had fallen into such a state of disrepair in a place like Mississippi, where cotton was still important to the economy.

"We are thinking of selling it," Dorothy said, pointing to the building.

"How long now it hasn't been used?" I asked. Cotton, and anything to do with it, is a reminder of the days of slavery. Undoubtedly, Dorothy didn't think about that. However, for someone like me whose heritage was rooted in slavery, a cotton mill was symbolic of the agony of the past, the legacy of several generations since abolition.

"Maybe twenty or so years ago, Grandfather decided a cotton mill was no place to have near to the home. He used to live here at that time. He closed it down built one on a plantation about a mile away."

"What do you want me to do?" I asked reluctantly.

"The first place to start would be to get rid of the grass. From there, you could see what needs to be done inside. Leave that for the last."

"Okay ma'am, I'll try to see what I can do with it."

"You will do a good job. During lunchtime, I may come over to keep you company, if you don't mind," she suggested.

"You think that's a good idea?" I asked, remembering once again our encounter that evening at the store.

"This is our land, private property…there's nothing to fear."

"What about your Grandfather?" I asked, wary about bringing up his name into our conversation. Dorothy was quite sensitive about her Grandfather.

"Oh! I didn't tell you this. The first day you came to work for us he was disappointed that you didn't start to work on cleaning up the mill. That's what he wanted you to do because of his intention to sell it."

"Hmm."

"I don't see any difference between now and then. As a matter of fact, I believe he would be glad to see you," she smiled.

"Will he be selling the house, too?" I asked, without any real reason for wanting to know.

"No, that's Ma's inheritance; it will be pass on to me and I'll pass it on to my children. If I don't have any…hmm, that would be something to think about," Dorothy giggled. "That small piece there behind it will be sold with it," she said, pointing in that direction.

"They were smart in constructing it away from the house," I said.

"I hate to say this; the truth is it was built by slaves years ago."

"I could easily have guessed that."

"Anyway, I have to run. Please don't worry about lunch. I will take you something."

Before I could raise any objection, Dorothy was well on her way to the back of the house. I tightened the grip on the machete that was handed to me, chopping away at the slender blades of grass that had every intention of taking over the outside of the mill. They just buckled under the sharp blade before falling to the ground.

Two hours into the task, sweat streamed down my face. The sun was not hot, a blessing in disguise. I could well imagine that in those slavery days my ancestors had to toil, enduring the miseries of plantation life under the watchful eyes of an overseer. Fortunately, for me, I had no eyes watching me. That was what I thought. I was wrong.

"You've been going great boy. Keep it up! Those are the hands I need to clean up this place," said the commanding voice of A.T. Pearsley from behind me.

I turned around to see him watching me with both arms akimbo. He wore a broad hat to shield his face from the sun. If it weren't for the voice, I might have had difficulty recognizing him at first.

"Thank you suh," I said quickly and continued to do what I was doing.

"You know if you weren't so stubborn, you could earn a lot of money around here. Your problem is boy you poke your nose where it doesn't belong," he lectured me.

I boiled with anger chopping harder to silence his voice. By so doing this could also help in getting rid of the steam building up in me.

"You do your work, you watch your step boy. Folks around here don't like strangers coming into town and..."

I was hoping he would have finished that thought. It might have given me a clue on how to sum up his behavior.

"...you remember not to bite the hand that feeds you. Remember that you hear me boy."

I kept on chopping away hearing his voice above the sound of the machete. I decided to stop after he was speaking no more. A.T. Pearsley had vanished mysteriously as he had come.

I was totally exhausted from that non-stop exercise. It was time for a break. My stomach started to make some noises. I got the message, so I walked over to a very leafy tree to sit on one of its bulging roots. I must have been there for about ten minutes before Dorothy walked up with a basket in her hand.

"I brought you something to eat. You must be starving," she said.

"You better believe I'm starving. I didn't have much to eat this morning.'

"Well here you go," Dorothy said, handing me a big bowl of stew.

"Whoa, when did you get time to cook this?" I asked, anxious to sample it.

"I did it early this morning. I left before lunchtime and went home to warm it up," she said, taking out her bowl.

"Your mother knows you are here?"

"Of course she does. She was the one who told me to make it."

"Hmm, that was nice of her," I said, unable to come up with any other response.

"My mother is a good woman. If she didn't allow her father to have so much influence over her, she would have been able to handle things much better."

"What do you mean?"

"As you can see, my Grandfather is a very peculiar man. They've lots of money. Their sin is they try to rule people's lives too much. That includes Ma and me," Dorothy said, putting down the bowl on the grass.

"She hasn't been able to stand up to her father eh?"

"She won't, she'll toe the line until they die. Ma and her brother stand to inherit a lot of money. I don't know what she's going to do with all that money."

"Forgive me for asking but what are some of the things your mother cannot do?"

"Ma would have remarried long ago. My Grandfather is against it thinking that anyone she marries would do so for the money."

"Can you blame him for that?" I asked, realizing that for once I agreed with A.T. Pearsley on something.

"It's not only that. If grandpa thinks Ma is seeing someone, he would do anything to prevent such a relationship."

"Is she seeing someone?" The stew tasted very good. I wanted to tell her that. The topic of the discussion was getting too interesting to change.

"Yes. I cannot say though. I'm the only one who knows although grandpa has been fishing around to find out."

"He was here today," I said, surprising her.

"What? What did he say?"

"The usual harsh words about doing what I'm paid to do. He also wants me to stop poking my nose into people's business whatever he means by that."

"Did he ask what you are doing here?" she said, curiosity in her voice.

"No, not at all. He spoke like he knew I would be working here," I assured her.

"I was right then," Dorothy smiled.

"You were right. By the way, this stew is good. You are a good cook, I must say."

"Thank you. If you allow me, I could let you taste some other things that I am good at," she grinned mischievously.

"Let us take it one day at a time," I suggested.

"Grandfather again?"

"Yes, I cannot deny that. I don't want to rock the apple cart."

"Here is an apple," she said, handing me one, "your statement is most timely."

"What's Uncle Bob doing at the store today?"

"He's trying to keep busy. Already, he misses you. I can see that. He's doing mostly packing, sorting out some fresh vegetables."

"He's a good man. He's concerned about me. All the troubles so far are giving him restless nights. I hope I can soon…"

"Leave for back east."

"Y-yes. I have no date planned. I came out here to take a break to make use of the opportunities around here. I hope my trip will be fruitful."

"I think it will be. From now on, things should be different. We'll get to know each other better, making life more interesting," Dorothy said with a laugh.

"You think it will be that easy?"

"Of course I do. Why shouldn't it be? All you have to do is stay far from Joe," she said, looking away from me.

"And the Klan."

Dorothy never expected to hear that name. An experience as the one we had that night was not so easily erased from memory, if it could be expunged at all.

"Yes, stay away from them. They're a force to be reckoned with. You and I won't be able to stop them."

"Do you think the colored folks around here know about them?" I asked, remembering how Benny had reacted to a similar question.

"They do. I think the attitude is let sleeping dogs lie."

"That's a nice way of putting it," I admitted. At the same time, I recognized the enormity of the problem and seriousness of the Klan's presence in any area where colored folks were living.

"I should be getting back to work now. Your Grandfather may be spying on us, or even Joe for that matter," I laughed.

Dorothy laughed, too. I recalled that night out into the woods with her. She had shown remarkable courage by going out there.

"You are a brave woman. Our trip that night will always be in my memory."

"There are some things that you do without thinking about them. I guess when you believe passionately that something is wrong you would do anything to prove it."

"I will hold you to that statement. That is a good way to end lunch,' I said.

"I can agree to that. You have a good afternoon. What time do you stop?" she asked, getting up to go.

"You tell me. I haven't even thought about that."

"For this kind of work 4 o'clock would be fine."

"I will see you tomorrow then."

"I will…dream about me tonight," she teased.

I smiled.

Uncle Bob was a very tired man when he came home at dusk. He didn't want anything to eat, mumbling something to the effect that he had stopped by Rebecca and had a very tasty stew.

I very much wanted to tell him that I, too, had tasted that stew and shared his view. He took out a letter from his pocket and handed it to me.

"I picked it up at the Post Office. I got one too."

"Thanks," I said, tearing the envelope quickly after seeing the Canadian stamp. It was from Grandma and Kate. I felt ashamed for not dropping them a line since I came here. Nevertheless, that didn't lessen my anxiety to read it.

My dear Luther,

I hope when these few lines reach you they will find you in the best of health. We are doing okay since you left. Lena comes when she can and she is helping out with almost everything. She is a good woman Luther. She keeps saying how much she misses you.

God is taking care of us and we know he is taking care of you too. Please take your time to do what you have to do. We know it is very important to you. Before you left we thought we were going to have a very difficult time, but Luther, God has been good to us. The crops will produce a very good harvest. We have already started to reap. If you have to stay there for the winter, we will be fine.

I hope you and Bob are getting along fine. You will because he is a like a lamb, a good man. Lena talks about you a lot and so does Kate. We all miss you son. Take care of yourself and please drop us a line to let us know what is happening with you. May God continue to bless you son. Remember to go to church every Sunday.

From Grandma, Kate and Lena

I read the letter three times. Tonight, I would sit to write a letter to them, no matter how long it would take me.

Shortly after I finished reading it, Benny and Maria were at the door. My heart pumped more blood when I saw them. They must have something to report.

"Are you all right?" I asked them.

"We are okay. Just felt bored in the house and decided to visit you folks," Benny said. "Of course Maria wouldn't miss out on such an opportunity with you being around," he laughed, confirming his good sense of humor. Sometimes, I tend to believe that under those comical statements was a grain of seriousness.

"Oh! I thought there was some development," I said, very disappointed.

"Cheer up son. All is not lost. We have to take it one day at a time. One day soon, we will be able to put our hands on some very vital information. Maria's friend Eva is certain she can get some more old newspapers for us. We have to wait and see," Benny said, watching Uncle Bob nodding in agreement.

"I'll see her on Friday. She may be able to get it by then," Maria said. "I saw her this morning and she promised me to do everything to get it."

"At least, I have something to look forward to this weekend," I said.

We talked for a while until it was time for them to go. My eyes were closing. I would have to fight sleep tonight; my pledge was to write that letter to grandma.

I was up until about midnight. I ended up writing what turned out to be three long pages. In addition, I wrote a separate letter to Lena. The room was taken over by Uncle Bob's snore at that hour.

Another two weeks went by quickly in Clarksville. Throughout that period, I accomplished nothing regarding the death of my father. My frustrations began to mount even before I was fully aware of that. Maria provided good company. That helped a lot. Eva's failure to get the old newspapers didn't make matters any better.

Dorothy had been getting much closer to me to try make real her own fantasies. What I wanted from her was proving to be an elusive dream. Jacob and A.T. Pearsley were either ignoring me, or trying to avoid me.

Many times I took up my bags with the conviction that it was time to go before the winter. We were well into the fall. The thought of returning to Canada and agonizing over my failure was not a welcome gesture to me. That bolstered my reason for deciding to stick it out to the end.

The only puzzling question I had was Uncle Bob. He neither encouraged nor discouraged me. It was not like the first week when I got here. I remembered his enthusiasm and excitement after I told him why I was here. I must have been rocking the boat too hard. He didn't say it though I needed no one to figure that out for me. Uncle Bob thought my approach was wrong in that I should leave the Pearsley's out of this. To him, they were respectable folks. Respected folks should be treated as such.

I had no quarrel with that except for one thing. Jacob and A.T. Pearsley should show respect for colored people. Respect is something to be earned. Believe me, with our tireless labor, forced and otherwise, we had earned every bit of it. We deserved to be shown that accordingly.

It was Thursday. I had finished the cleaning of the cotton mill concentrating more now on the cellar. According to Dorothy, there was a lot of cleaning to do down there. I better brace myself for that, she told me.

I was on my way to take on that task when Tim Barker pulled up beside me in his almost brand new car. It was so glossy that I could see myself along the side facing me.

"Good morning young man, what are you up to now? Are you working?" he asked, a fat cigar sticking out of his mouth. Tim Barker was not a handsome man. There was too much flesh on his face and under his chin. Tim was too heavy despite the fact that he could have a challenging time taking off some of that fat. To make matters worse, he stood no more than about five feet six inches.

"I am suh." I grumbled.

"Oh! You are. I was about to tell you that I could give you a job if you want one. I could do with another hand at the back of the store," he said, almost blowing the curly blue smoke into my face. That could have been deliberate though it was difficult for me to conclude.

"Thanks suh. I don't know how long I'll be at this one. I could let you know as soon as it's over."

"Well, it will be there waiting for you. Stay out of trouble boy," Tim said. He drove off before I could answer.

I had to give credit where credit was due. If it were up to Tim, I would not have been thrown in jail a month ago. He allowed Joe to bully him into believing I had actually stole something from the store. As for his job offer, I was in no hurry to take him up on that one.

Dorothy and Rebecca were on their way to work when I got there. They could not stop to talk with me. That was all right. I knew what to do, consequently I wasted no time in doing that.

The cellar was in one mess. I could not understand how they could have lived there and allow it to become a huge garbage dump. Everything they didn't want, the cellar was the ideal place for storage. I stood there surveying the mess, not knowing where to begin.

Surprisingly, I had expected it to be very dark. There was a kind of window that was neatly fitted just above ground. The rays of the sun squeezed themselves through it providing enough light for me to do some work. I left the cellar door open and that also made a big difference.

Boxes were piled on top of each other; broken furniture, chairs, tables, beds, were all leaning on each other for support. The dusty floor was bed for broken crockery, glass, and even pictures.

I decided it would be best to start at the entrance work my way inwards close to the back of the room. By so doing it would be less cumbersome to manouevre around all that junk.

At the end of the day, I was deadbeat. The only break I took was thirty minutes for lunch. Uncle Bob passed by some minutes after five o'clock on his way home. That was the time I realized the workday was done. I had been so involved in what I was doing.

"Yuh have one heck of a job there son," he said, coming down the stairs leading to the cellar.

"You can say that again," I replied. "No tornado hasn't passed by recently?"

"We had a big one last year. Why? You mean no one has been here for a while?"

"Exactly. This is in a big mess."

"Come, Rebecca says we should stay for supper," he grinned. "She believes it is so bad down here that you'll need a special meal to recover."

And a special meal it was too. I spent fifteen minutes getting rid of the dust. I was placed before a nice slab of beef roast, potatoes and vegetables. It did not dawn on me how hungry I was until the smell serenaded my nose. While the rest of the table spoke, I ate all I could.

"My goodness! You were starving," Dorothy exclaimed. "I should have brought you lunch today."

"That's okay, I enjoy my meal if I'm starving," I said.

"I can well imagine the tough task you have to do down there," Rebecca said.

"Indeed ma'am, it's a lot of work."

"Take your time, there's no hurry to finish. You deserve a big bonus at the end of this job," she said.

"It would be wise to finish before winter sets in," Dorothy suggested.

"What the winters are like here?" I asked.

"It does get cold nowhere like the east, I can assure you," Rebecca said.

"We could sell you snow," I joked, remembering right away that I dare not call the name Canada.

"You're getting a lot of snow out there now? Dorothy asked.

I saw Uncle Bob giving me the eye. I got the cue that he was reminding me to watch my tongue. There was no room for a slip of the tongue now.

"Sometimes the winters give us more snow than we can imagine ma'am."

"How much longer will you be around?" Rebecca asked.

"I had planned to be back before winter. You folks are keeping me busy which I'm grateful for. I may leave right after the winter. I have to get some seeds into the ground when spring arrives."

"It is a pity you won't be around here. The planting season here is a busy place," she replied.

"Maybe the next time I come it will be in the spring."

Dorothy's eyes never left me. Obviously, she was not pleased with whatever I was saying. My guess was she was hoping I could stay indefinitely.

"What's your father like?" Rebecca asked.

There was silence in the room. Not even the eating utensils were making any noise. Uncle Bob was frozen; Dorothy picked at her food. Me, I used the plate to get my attention. I didn't have much time to think about what I was going to say. Yet I had to say the right thing.

"My father works very hard. He loves the field."

"Like his brother," Rebecca grinned.

I felt better now. "We work together on the farm, feeding the cows, horses and a few chickens."

"What about your mother?" Dorothy asked.

Having grown up with my Grandmother, I could easily answer that question. "My mother ensures we have enough to eat. She helps out with the planting in the spring too."

"You should all visit some day," Rebecca said. "You and Bob are the only two members of the family that I know. When you return tell them how nice it is over here," Rebecca said.

"Yes ma'am."

"That will have to be planned a long time in advance," Uncle Bob said, his voice cracking.

"I know. It would be so nice to have them here," Rebecca said.

"If they cannot come, we can go one of these days," Dorothy said.

My heart jumped. What were they getting into? The sooner we could change this conversation, the better it would be for me. Uncle Bob was stirring in his seat, a sign of his discomfort.

"We will see what happens," I said.

"I always want to go to New York," Dorothy said.

I didn't even know I was supposed to come from New York. I kept saying east. With New York being touted now, I was confused.

"New York is nice although we are far from the cities," I said.

"Have you ever been to New York City?" Dorothy asked.

"One time, when I was small. I don't remember it."

"You should go again. Maybe when we come we could all go together. My dream is to go there."

"That is something to think about," I said, trying to sound as credible as possible. Uncle Bob was getting so nervous he had stopped eating.

"That was good Rebecca," Uncle Bob interjected. "Thanks for saving us the trouble of cooking tonight."

"You know you're always welcome here," she said.

"It has been a long day," he said briskly.

"Yes. Luther must be tired."

"I am," I replied, glad for the opportunity to get out of the tense conversation.

We left them standing at the doorway; their eyes trailed us as we made our way through the gate.

"They almost had us there eh?" Uncle Bob said on our way home.

"I saw your sign and was very careful in whatever I was about to say. Do you think they suspect anything?"

"Oh no, I believe they genuinely want to go for a visit."

"How do you feel about that?"

"You know that's not possible. We have to avoid that all we can. If that conversation ever comes up again, we have to try to find a way to get rid of it," he said emphatically. Uncle Bob was serious about what he had said; his fist was clenched and he kept nodding in disapproval.

"We may have to avoid those suppers while I am here," I suggested.

"That's a good idea. When the two of us are together it is likely that the discussion will come up again."

"I find it interesting that Rebecca insists on meeting the family."

"Huh, she's always like that. From I met her, she has been saying that. I'm always trying to avoid the conversation. By the way, how are you and Maria getting on these days?" he asked, changing the subject.

For a moment, I thought that maybe it was a deliberate strategy not to talk too much about Rebecca. I could be wrong though I hardly think so.

"We're doing fine. Maria is a very nice lady. I am surprised she's single," I said, waiting for his reaction.

"She's one of those women who's trying to find Mr. Perfect," he grinned at me.

"I suppose I'm like you. If you don't mind me asking, what stopped you from getting married?"

I could not see the reaction on his face. It was almost dark, the few remaining rays of sun had already been swallowed by darkness. "You know son, when Caleb died, a part of me went too. I saw no need for getting married, only to take care of my existing one. I haven't been able to do that well, I must admit. After all these years, I haven't given up. Are you seeing anyone in Canada?"

"Yes, there's someone waiting for me - Lena. You couldn't want a nicer woman. I hope she'll have the patience to wait for me," I said sincerely.

"She will, you don't worry about that. I can tell you that Maria is very interested. She must know that someone with your characteristics don't go around alone."

"Did she discuss me with you?" I asked curiously.

"Not exactly, however, your name came up in conversations. Huh, Maria seems to be crazy over you."

"Just like Dorothy…"

Uncle Bob stopped right there in his tracks. He started to walk again after a brief pause. To say he was stunned was no exaggeration.

"What are you talking about son?" he asked. "You playing games, you serious about what you just said?"

"I'm not playing games uncle. I wouldn't do such a thing with something like this."

"I have a hunch you is serious," he said stopping again. "I'm the one who is refusing to believe it."

"Why?" I asked, resuming our walk.

"This is the state of segregation son. Do you know what you is getting into eh? It's hard son…hard to prevent a woman from going after you. As a man, there is something you can do. I'm telling you from experience son."

"Experience."

"Yes. Keep far from her…don't be with her alone. Please don't encourage anything. That's all I can say now. It's against the law here," Uncle Bob said harshly.

Was Uncle Bob a coward, or was he merely concerned about me?

"I want to tell you that I haven't been encouraging anything. If I were, we would be deep into a relationship by now."

"She has been tempting to start one?"

"Eh-huh."

"If her mother ever know, not to mention her Grandfather, all hell would break loose. Her uncle would go crazy," he growled in disapproval.

"Like what?"

"I don't even want to think about it," he said. "Let us rest this argument. We shouldn't even be having this talk now. Something like this should be far from us, not even entering our minds."

"Are you that fearful?" I asked, feeling as if I was forced to do so.

"One day I will tell you why," he said, opening the front door to the house.

On Friday morning, I was back at it down in the cellar. For most of the morning, I was getting rid of old cardboard boxes. There was a pile of them stacked in one corner. The very last one at the bottom was different from the others that were on top of it.

For one, it was much bigger with some strings wrapped around it. At first, I thought nothing about it and I continued to get rid of all the others. The moment I stood over that box I realized that it was an important piece of junk. Apart from the fact that it was at the bottom, it was carefully sealed, the side of it was torn open, possibly by a huge bounce.

The contents of the box raised my curiosity. What appeared to be a piece of paper was sticking out of the side. The paper turned out to be some photographs. There must have been about a dozen.

I carefully pulled them out leaving the vacant spot that they occupied. I did not want to open the box from the top in the event that I was accused of tampering with it. There were other pictures in the box.

I glanced at the pictures in my hand. The first one I saw was that of a white family posing before an automobile – apparently a newly bought one. There were about three others similar to that one. The next picture was that of a man whipping a colored man. I was so frightened the picture almost fell out of my hand.

I picked it up from the dusty floor, examined it closer, but I could not see the face of the man being beaten. The white man didn't look familiar either. He was young making it useless for me to identify him unless someone could identify him for me.

The find was getting more interesting, making me put three of the boxes together to make a seat. I had never seen any pictures actually taken of a whipping. The person was down on his knees apparently pleading while the man with the whip had somewhat of a grin on his face.

Reluctantly, I put that picture away and took up another one. The next one was even more horrible. A colored man was being dragged in the streets with his hands tied behind him. A crowd of onlookers watched in the distance.

What was all this about? I began to ask myself. Having come this far, I had no alternative but to look further. I must be prepared to see what was ahead. There were more pictures; with the pictures came more stories.

Again, the next picture was another white man standing beside his car. I flipped over the back and the name "Jacob" was scribbled on it. I looked at the back of the others I had seen. There was nothing written on them.

The picture beneath that one was simply that of burning wood – nothing else but burning wood. That was what I thought first, however, on closer examination, I could see a campfire. A campfire…the Klan? My thoughts stopped there as soon as my eyes caught the next picture. I turn my eyes away from it wondering if I should really look at it.

The picture made me sick in my stomach. I felt churning, burning, and groaning. I wanted to see it; yet something was telling me to stuff it back into the box and forget all about it. Suppose it was something I should not see? Suppose it would add more to my pain than alleviate the grief of not knowing who were the people responsible for lynching my father? Could these pictures provide the lead I needed to make a break in our little probe?

I prayed to God to give me strength to confront what my eyes were about to behold. While I did not take a long, hard, look on the picture,

I knew what was there. I saw the haunting image flashed by my eyes the moment I removed the one that was on top of it. It was then I looked away.

Slowly and calmly, I fixed my eyes on the picture before me. A colored man dangled from the end of a rope. About a dozen people were looking up at him. Beside the man, a horse was drinking water nearby.

For five minutes, my eyes never left the picture. As one would imagine, the only question on my lips was: Could this be my father?" While in Canada, I had often expressed regret of not even having a picture of my father. Could this be him?

Some parts of the picture were grainy. This picture was taken early morning when the sun was not that bright. The face of the man resembled a ball with rough edges. There were no distinguishing features.

I peered at it until water came into my eyes. It was futile; the picture was old and crumpled. The person with the camera must have been far from the scene.

I ran my fingers through the remaining pictures to see if there was any other like it. There was none. Funny, I thought. Carefully, I put the pictures back from where I had taken them. If I were to be charged for theft of a picture, I was willing to do that. In my mind, I was not stealing. Somehow, I would replace this picture when I was through with it. For now, I needed it because it was crucial to my mission here.

Was this providence or coincidence? I was sent to clean this cellar. Here in my hand was something that could turn out to be a valuable piece of evidence, proof or what have you, regarding the death of my father. Although I could not recognize anyone in the picture, that didn't mean it was not valuable.

I left work an hour earlier. I went to the school that Maria taught. It was a small one-room school tucked away on the outskirts of town. It was an elementary school. To my chagrin, all the children I saw crammed into that room were colored. I had never confronted segregation before. Now it was right before my eyes.

I made my presence known to Maria and then waited outside until school was dismissed. One thing I could say about the children was that they seemed eager to learn. For about a minute I watched them in class. Their eyes were glued on Maria, waiting for each word that proceeded from her mouth.

"You have a good class," I told her as soon as the children disappeared in all directions. The other teacher, who assisted her, was busy tidying up the classroom.

"Luther, thank you, it's so good to see you out here. I have never had anyone coming to meet me at school," she laughed aloud.

"There will always be a first. I'm glad I'm the first in this case."

"Is everything all right?"

"Hmm. I don't want you to interpret this wrongly. I was doing some work at Rebecca's, and deciding to stop earlier than usual."

"Something happened?" she asked, stopping in the pathway to look back at the school. The other teacher was still inside.

"Is she going to be there for long?" I asked.

"No, in a few minutes she'll leave. It's her week to clean up. We usually do it alternately."

"Oh, I see. I thought I would come to see you. The truth is I have more than one reason to do that."

"Well, please spell them out," she teased. "I am listening."

"I was cleaning out some garbage in the cellar. I came across a box with some photographs. The box was torn. I saw this picture along with some others," I said, handing it to her.

Maria hadn't seen me with the picture. I had it wrapped in a piece of paper. She took it from me so reluctantly that she must have guessed that it had to be of utmost importance.

I studied her face closely. There was a frown followed by wrinkles across her forehead. She moved the picture closer to her eyes examining it carefully.

"This is awful…" Her hand dropped to her side with the picture in it. "Oh!…L-Luther, what is this…who…" She looked at me wanting to suggest something that I hadn't yet brace myself to ask.

"That is the question Maria, who's this poor man?"

"There were other pictures?" she asked.

"Yes."

"My goodness! Are you thinking…" she said coming closer to me.

"It is possible. I don't know whom else to show it to. They don't know I have this particular picture."

"You don't need to show it anyone…at least not yet. Let it be known only to the two of us," Maria suggested.

"That's a good idea. The time for anyone else to know isn't yet," I said nodding my head in approval.

"There's another secret I want to share with you," Maria said, as we walked on.

"Yeah. It must be a day of secrets."

"I have my little secret, and been nurturing and petting for quite some time now."

"I'm anxious." I was anxious. If my guess was right, her secret was something I could not handle right now. Not with what was unfolding at this time.

"I'm crazy about you Luther. Sometimes I wish you would never solve this case - not for now. That means you'll be here until you probably change your mind about returning for Canada," she said, slipping her hand into mine.

I held her hand for the fun of it. I don't think it meant anything serious on my part. At the same time, I didn't want to send the wrong signals. Lena had left an impression on me that would be very hard to change. For now, I wished it remained that way because only absence or time could change that. On the contrary, I couldn't state that position to Maria at this moment; the timing was far off.

"I have always seen it in your eyes," I said softly.

Maria released my hand turning around quickly to face me. "Why didn't you tell me? I'm here torturing myself alone!" she exclaimed.

"It's nice to know someone feels that way Maria. As I explained before, the time isn't right for this. Who knows, I could soon be gone and you will be left broken hearted? Please don't get me wrong Maria. You are a wonderful woman, a beautiful one, too. Let's take it one day at a time until we see what happens," I said calmly.

I had expected Maria to be angry. Her response was far from that.

And that was why I admired her so much. "Like I said before, I have a lot of patience. If I have to wait, I will," she smiled. "Thanks for those kind words."

She held my hand again. We walked toward home full of hope that the coming weeks could provide answers to many of our questions.

All day Saturday, my mind was on that picture. Each opportunity I got, I took it from my pocket, scrutinize it carefully, trying to get my eyes familiar with the blurred face of the victim that was hanged.

On Sunday, after services Maria said she had something very important to tell me. I thought she had done that yesterday. What else could that be?

Uncle Bob was with Benny. We went outside under a tree.

"Here, take a look," she said. "I find this very amazing, if not coincidental. Eva Simms, remember my friend whose Mama is the Librarian in Clarksville, she finally came up with something."

Maria placed a piece of old newspaper in my hand. My eyes felt like they were going to pop out of my head. In the picture, a colored man was being hanged right under a tree near water. Furthermore, there were some onlookers.

"My God," I said, not meaning to take the name of the Lord in vain in violation of the third commandment, but to give him thanks for giving us this important bit of information. The writing below the picture said: *"Caleb Nesbeth dangling from a rope early yesterday morning after he was taken from jail by a mob and hanged for attempting to murder a well-known businessman in Clarksville."*

My knees wobbled under me. I was going to faint. I lowered my body to the protruding root of the tree in order to sit. My head felt light, nausea overcame me and I started to sweat. There was a striking similarity to the picture I found in the cellar. It was unbelievable that both pictures could surface almost at the same time.

Maria held my hand tightly. "Take it easy…take it easy Luther…just sit…just sit…"

Tears rolled down my face. Through teary eyes, I saw Maria's wet face. We held onto each other for support, preferring to remain in that position until we regained our composure. We didn't speak, we just sat there looking at the picture. My groaning was deep down within me. Even though it happened long ago, the grief of death was as fresh as this morning's dew. It was for the father I never knew. It was for the father I always yearned for – the missing link in my life all these years.

The picture in the newspaper did not show his face clearly because it was hanging down with his chin resting on the knotted noose. His limp body could not provide any hint of what he was like before his demise. All that didn't matter now. What mattered was who were the people responsible for taking the law into their own hands – murder. A number of names popped up before me.

Chapter Eleven

Maria told me Eva wanted the picture back, because it was very important to the Library's archives. However, she didn't give a deadline to return it. I perfectly understood that and pledged to return it as soon as I no longer needed it.

Uncle Bob said he had to take some bills that he had for Maria, following an errand yesterday. I told him I wanted to go home to get some rest to prepare for another tiring day tomorrow. That was okay with him. Benny and Maria had to visit someone requiring them to leave church early.

Overhead, the sky opened up as a long streak of lightning divided the heavens in the flash of a second. Thunder shook the valley with a force that made me shiver. Huge raindrops tumbled out of the sky splattering onto the dusty surface of the road on the way home. The smell of dust permeated the vicinity, as the rains poured with a vengeance on dry ground.

I started to run. Clutching my Bible with the piece of newspaper inside it, my feet appeared to be almost touching my hands. I had never stretched my leg in such a long time. What I had in my hand was too precious – too precious to get wet, both the Bible and the newspaper.

By the time I reached home, I was out of breath. I turned the key in the door quickly and ran inside. I sat around the table for a few minutes breathing harder than any racing horse.

A few minutes later, I took out the piece of newspaper again. There was a story relating to the picture. The headline read: "LYNCHING IN CLARKSVILLE."

The story continued: "*Shortly before sunrise yesterday, a colored man was hauled out of the county jail by an angry mob and hanged minutes later.*

Caleb Nesbeth was arrested earlier in the day, after he allegedly stabbed a businessman and robbed him of an undisclosed sum of money. An eyewitness reported seeing Nesbeth standing over store-owner William Hay with a knife in hand.

Reports say Nesbeth, who worked at Hay's General Store as well as on a nearby farm, was caught as he tried to leave town. He was taken to jail and a trial was expected soon. However, an angry mob raided the jail early yesterday, gagged the Sheriff, and took Nesbeth to the outskirts of town and hanged him.

I wanted to read no more. I had had enough. Now that I had established the fact that he was dragged from jail and executed, I must now proceed to try to answer some of the questions lingering in my mind. For example, who was the witness? Who truly committed that murder? Apparently, the motive was robbery. If it was not, what was the real motive?

Uncle Bob got home around eight o'clock. He must have had supper over by Rebecca because he went straight to bed. I didn't say anything about the newspaper. I was already in bed, pretending to be sleeping. The images on the picture haunted my mind utilizing all the energy I had to think about something else.

The next morning, I woke up to find myself hugging my pillow – something I had never done before. My dream last night rushed into my thoughts with the force of a storm. My father told me in a very puzzling way that he was troubled with something he himself could not figure out. Dreams can be mysterious and unexplainable at times. They make reality seems far-fetched - an illusion themselves. Whereas, for us, dreams are essentially that – dreams, not reality.

My dream was like an incomplete crossword puzzle where you don't know where or how to make the next move. I decided not to occupy my time trying to interpret what my father was saying. Firstly, I was not an interpreter of dreams, it could be merely mind over matter.

Uncle Bob didn't speak about his whereabouts after church. He told me he had to get to work early to catch upon his work, especially since I was not there to help. I could see why he didn't have any time to find out more about my father's death.

I left the house right after Uncle Bob walking straight to Rebecca's house – straight into the grinning face of Mighty Joe. He was standing by Rebecca in anticipation of my arrival.

"Good morning," I said, addressing both of them.

"Good morning Luther," Rebecca replied.

Joe did not say anything.

"Luther, Joe is going to finish the cellar for us. He started to clean it up last year. He heard you were doing it but want to finish the job he started," Rebecca said.

As far as I could remember, no work had started in cleaning up that cellar, unless the mess started to pile up again. That could have been so, though unlikely. I smelled a rat somewhere.

"That is okay with me," I said right away. "If he's as good as his mouth, he'll do a better job than me."

"You son of…" Joe said, making a step toward me.

"Pleeease stop it!" Rebecca screamed on top of her voice. Joe backed off while I stood there laughing to myself. A poor young man like me didn't have much say in this. I was a hired hand that could be given notice at anytime. Unknown to my employers, I got a precious gift from them – that picture of my father.

I was careful to put back the others as I had found them. My fervent hope was for them not to discover the missing one.

"We will pay you for the rest of the week," Rebecca said.

Joe did not like that; his face changed color. He wanted to say something. Instead he chose to remain silent.

"Thanks ma'am."

"I will give Bob your pay on Friday."

"Thank you ma'am," I said and walked away. Another development in the case, I thought. Were the chickens coming home to roost? I was very positive that if that was a wager, I could win it.

I had nothing else planned for the rest of the day, except for a quiet moment somewhere. There was no better place else than Cold Stream. It was quiet as usual, the refreshing air of autumn diluted with a winter chill, blew through the park.

Right away, I started to rattle my brain. Why did Mighty Joe have so much interest in finishing up with the cleaning of that cellar? And that was if he wanted to do that any at all. Something was going on. The way things had been going it was only a matter of time before I had the answer.

Over supper, a rather subdued Uncle Bob picked at his food. He had lost his appetite. I didn't have to guess the answer to that. Earlier, I had told him what happened at Rebecca's.

"It all seems confusing son. One moment you is at the store, another time you is in jail. Yet another time yuh is no longer working at Rebecca's. What is going on?"

"Hmm, I've been asking myself that question too. And I think I know why," I replied.

"Why son?"

"I believe some of what's happening has to do with my father. Don't ask me how because I haven't been able to verify it. I will though," I nodded with confidence.

Uncle Bob reached across the table and hold my arm. "Do you really think that it is. I don't think so," he said shaking his head. "We are coloreds…I have lived with that long enough to know when the race question is rearing its ugly head son."

"You could be right. These are my thoughts, I may be dead wrong," I said knowing fully well that it was exactly the opposite. My reason for doing that was to free Uncle Bob of any concern or reservation he might have about the way things have been going in my mission.

"Before you start any little work again, be sure of what you is getting into son. It's a funny place around these parts."

With that, we retired to bed. I was totally debilitated, maybe from exercising my brain. It didn't take me long to fall asleep.

The next day I stayed at home, catching up on some sleep, planning a strategy to deal with whatever the outcome would be of my mission.

At dusk, Benny and Maria came home with Uncle Bob. They decided it was time to get together to have another discussion about our achievements so far. As we were about to begin, there was a tap on the door. I opened it to see the obese frame of Mighty Joe loomed in the shadows of early evening.

Uncle Bob invited him in before I could say anything.

"I'm not staying. I came to clear up a matter," he said stone-faced.

"What matter?" Uncle Bob asked, looking up into his face.

I was ninety percent certain his visit had something to do with me. I was right.

Joe rolled his eyes on me. "This young nephew of yours has been causing a lot of trouble ever since he came here," Joe claimed.

"You know that's not true," Maria snapped, anger in her voice.

"I wasn't speaking to you," Joe snapped. "Speak when you are spoken to."

"You cannot speak to my daughter like that, you slob," Benny said, rising to his feet. "This isn't even your house; it is owned by a colored man. The likes of you shouldn't be even near it!" Benny snapped back.

"Gentlemen!" Uncle Bob bellowed.

"It's not yours either," Joe shouted back.

"I'm a more welcomed guest than you," Benny shouted in anger.

"What's the purpose of your visit?" Uncle Bob asked, trying to quell the harsh exchange of words.

"This boy here has something that doesn't belong to him," Joe said.

Up to this point I had said nothing.

"His name is Luther," Benny corrected him.

"Boy for me," he said sarcastically.

"What's it that he has for you?" Uncle Bob asked.

"He has a picture that was taken from Rebecca's cellar," Joe said.

"Picture? What picture? There ain't no picture here…no picture. What kinda picture? If he had a picture I would have seen it," Uncle Bob said.

"Where's the picture?" he demanded.

"Get the hell out of this house!" I said angrily. "This is our house. How dare you come here to make such an accusation?"

Joe's face was flushed with anger. I want him to swallow the bait because there was no way he was going to get that picture."

"Go! Go! Go!" Benny said flashing his hand at him. "We can do well without someone like you around here."

"You'll hear from the Sheriff," Joe said, walking through the door.

"If you believe you are going to do what you did to him the other day you are making a sad mistake...a very big one," Benny said, not backing down from his very brave stance.

"Is that a threat?" Joe asked.

"Take it however you want," Benny shouted back.

Joe went through the door slamming it behind him.

"They think they have all the power in this country. It is time we begin to stand up for our rights," Benny said. "We have to start battling for civil rights."

"Thanks," I said.

"What was he talking about?" Uncle Joe asked.

I went into my room for the picture and newspaper clipping. Returning with the picture, I threw them down on the table. Benny and Uncle Bob hesitated before taking them up together.

"By golly," Uncle Bob said. "I'll be damned! They almost look alike."

"I cannot believe it...it cannot be," Benny said. "This is Caleb!" That's him...my goodness!" he said slowly.

"How did you know?" I asked, knowing that the story below explained it all. They did not start to read the story rather their eyes were searching the pictures.

"The plaid shirt," he said pointing at it. "The same shirt I saw him in jail with the day he was arrested."

"You found it at Rebecca's? Eva found the newspaper too." Uncle Bob asked.

"I found the picture in the cellar."

"I don't blame you for not telling that redneck," Benny said, referring to Joe. "He's just one heap of trash."

"The story below explains it all," Maria said.

"What do we do now?" I asked.

"I suggest you don't keep this picture here," Benny said.

"Do I have a choice?" I asked.

"We'll keep it," Benny offered. "That rascal is so bitter that he may very well take the Sheriff here."

"I think that you keeping them is a good idea," Uncle Bob said.

"We'll hold them for a while. There'll be no rush right now. There's something very interesting about them," Benny said.

"What's that?" I asked.

"You see those men standing near to the horse," he said pointing to them. "It will be interesting to find out who they are."

I didn't notice those men before in any great detail. "That will be a tough nut to crack."

"I need to think. Give me a few days," Benny replied.

To have someone like Rebecca come to your home is cause for alarm. As close as she is to Uncle Bob, she never visits our house. On Wednesday morning she did, before Uncle Bob could leave for work.

"Sorry to wake you up gentlemen. This is a surprise visit," she said. Rebecca was nervous.

"What is it?" I asked dryly.

"The picture. Did you take a picture as Joe claims? I don't expect you would ever do something like that. The picture is important, it belongs to the family. We wouldn't want to lose it - something as personal as a picture."

Uncle Bob looked at me.

"Why would you think I would do something like that? I asked.

"That man has been causing so much trouble for Luther since he came here," Uncle Bob said, with some amount of difficulty. "What's going on Rebecca?"

"I'm sorry. I have to go. Bob, you can stay home today. Please don't come back until we need you." Rebecca didn't wait for our reaction. She walked away quickly, vanishing like an apparition.

"Wait!" Uncle Bob shouted. "Wait, Rebecca! Can you explain what's going on?"

Rebecca didn't even look back. Uncle Bob made a step forward. He moved no further.

"Son, we are stepping into uncharted waters. I don't know what we are getting into now. Maybe we should call off this thing."

I was amazed at that statement. In one sense, I should not be surprised. Of late, Uncle Bob had been showing lack of interest in what I had been doing. I was getting too excited now. There was hardly anything that could stop me now, barring sickness or death.

"Now isn't the time to stop," I said. "We have come too far for that Uncle Bob. I want to get it over with and return to Canada."

Uncle Bob studied my face. I saw the pain in his eyes. Undoubtedly, he was disappointed with what Rebecca had told him.

"If that is how you feel I know I won't be able to stop you. This is something dear to you. I know that son."

"Rebecca doesn't seem to be of her own mind. I am sorry about what she told you a while ago," I said, walking to the back of the house with him.

"Maybe it's a good thing. I need to be able to survive on my own. The only problem is that it comes at a bad time with winter around the corner. I can survive. Rebecca will call me back as soon as this pressure is over," he said, forcing a smile.

"Where there's life there is hope. If God is for us who can be against us," I reminded him.

"True son, wise words. Benny is at home, let us go and look him up," Uncle Bob suggested.

We walked over to Benny's house to find him chopping firewood. Maria was at school.

"Is something wrong? I shouldn't be asking that, I know something is wrong. You should be at work now," Benny said.

"Rebecca told me a few minutes ago that she doesn't need me right now. She did that to me two years ago y'know; it is nothing new," Uncle Bob said, trying to sound upbeat.

"Oh, I got word last night that Ol' Titus wants to see us now."

I clenched my fist in triumph. "Good! Good! That is good news, when can we see him?" I asked, my hand still clasped in a ball.

"Whenever we want," he replied.

"We have the time now. We should make use of it," Uncle Bob said.

"That's true Uncle Bob."

"How about tomorrow afternoon? There's something I have to do this afternoon," Benny said.

"That's fine with me," I said.

"He may have something that we want to hear. The faster we can get some more information the better," Benny said.

All three of us went to sit down beneath a tree at the back. Benny had a nice, neat looking house that was big enough for he and Maria. Benny had lost his wife a few years ago.

"And what are we going to do with the information should we get anything substantial?" Uncle Bob asked.

"Here's the plan," Benny said, using a piece of stick to draw some lines on the gravel surface to illustrate his point. "I am suggesting, and Maria agrees, that as soon as we gather the evidence we head straight for the District Attorney's office in Jackson. We ain't gonna go to no lawman in this town. They are all a bunch of yellowbelly cowards."

"Do you think we can do that?" Uncle Bob asked.

"Why not? If he asked why we will tell him there's no justice here."

"We have the newspaper…if only we could find that witness. We don't even know if it's a man or a woman. That witness knows the truth, imagine that," I said, trying to radiate a ray of hope that we would eventually find the mystery witness.

We chatted all morning. At noon, Benny made us some lunch and we compensated for that by helping him to finish chopping the wood. Maria would soon be home; I decided I would go to meet her.

Once again, she was surprised to see me. "Has something happened again?" she asked as we left school for home.

"Rebecca came over this morning to ask me about the picture. She also told Uncle Bob to stay put for a while."

"To stop working? What did you tell her about the picture?"

"I didn't give a direct answer."

"How is Uncle Bob taking it? I don't understand how she could do such a thing to him. They have been going around for so long…" Maria said something she shouldn't have – too late. By the time she realized that the words had already left her lips. If she could have taken back that last sentence, she would have done that. She knew I was waiting for a further explanation. I stopped in my tracks staring at her.

"You mean you didn't know?" she asked, as we both stopped in the middle of the road.

"Know what?"

"I'm sorry I shouldn't have said that. Let's us forget it," she said, walking again.

I held my ground. Maria saw I was not following her. She turned to face me.

"Okay, I think I know you by now. Rebecca and Uncle Bob have been seeing each other...under wraps, for many years now, shortly after her husband died," she said, watching for my reaction.

"Apart from you, who else knows this?"

"Dad and Dorothy."

"And you are positive about that?"

"Very positive. In this segregated town, if that word ever gets around there could be problems. It is against the law."

We started to walk again. "How are they able to do this without the nosy Jacob finding out?"

"I don't have a clue. I believe Rebecca asks him to take things to the house. He use that opportunity to see her."

"How did you know about the relationship?"

"We're very close to Uncle Bob. He confides in us...he told us."

"Hmm, is Rebecca that desperate that he would take such a chance?"

"The racial problem in this state is very serious. She should know better than that. We told Uncle Bob to try to get out of the relationship. He says its hard because he feels obligated to her."

"The job is making him feel obligated. If that Joe ever gets a hint that something like that is happening, I hate to think what would happen to poor Uncle Bob," I said, suddenly weighing the seriousness of the matter.

"Not to mention her father...Jacob too," she added.

"Phew, I'm getting nervous now," I admitted.

"Don't you worry your head about that. It's been going on for years now. He'll get his job back because Rebecca cannot do without him for long. I believe her father or Jacob pressured her into doing that."

"That's why Uncle Bob took the job loss so easy. Hmm, they must be going crazy about that picture."

"Did you hear Ol' Titus wants to see us now?" she asked.

"I'm thrilled. I hope he doesn't disappoint us."

"All we have to do is wait and see."

"How does Dorothy feel about this relationship?" I asked, thinking how Uncle Bob had dropped several hints about not getting involved with Dorothy. He knew what he had gotten into and didn't want me following in his footsteps.

"I can't say. Uncle Bob hasn't said anything about her. It's hard to tell," she said, grabbing onto my arm.

"I don't think she's in opposition to that kind of relationship."

"Why do you say that?" Maria asked.

My thinking cap was on already. Caution had to be taken in answering that question. "Dorothy likes everyone, black or white, pink or blue."

"Are you trying to tell me something?" she asked, maintaining her grip on my forearm.

"No, not at all."

"…Like how Dorothy has been trying to get your attention," she said jokingly.

"You are guessing now, eh?"

"Sometimes when you guess it turns out to be the correct answer."

"I guess…I am guessing too, that even if Dorothy likes me, it's almost useless. Why would I want to live in fear for the rest of my life?"

"How?

"Interracially…the KKK, the stares, the comments, the law. I couldn't live with that for a day," I replied very confidently.

"Money can buy love in some circumstances. I have heard of it, I have seen it happen."

"In my case it won't," I told her.

Maria stopped to plant a kiss on my cheeks. We headed toward home holding hands together.

We had planned on visiting Ol' Titus this afternoon at around four o'clock. That was roughly four hours away. With nothing much to do, I walked slowly to Cold Stream to kill the remaining hours.

Cold Stream was as beautiful as ever. The sound of water running over rocks and vegetation was pleasant to hear again. My thoughts strayed back to Canada, the people that were important to me there – Kate, Grandma and Lena. They must be missing me. I could not deny that after nearly five months that my yearnings to return had become more frequent. My patience had been running out. Nevertheless, I had to hang on a bit longer for the sake of my father's name.

My confidence was growing each day. These things were happening to me could not be coincidental. At nights, I had nightmares about finding out the truth. As soon as I came back to reality, all I could think about was bringing my father's killers to justice. I had reached a level of obsession that only a positive outcome could get rid of it. And even after that, often times I wonder if I could have a future in the growing civil rights movement. From this mission, I could see I have a knack for anything to do with equality and justice issues.

I slid off the rock I was sitting onto the grass, where I stretched out flat on my back. I yawned loudly, as if I was near my bedtime. That was far away. I started to whistle - something I had not done for a while now.

"I didn't know you could whistle that good," said a voice a few seconds later.

Dorothy stood looking over me. Her inverted image still couldn't hide the laugh on her face.

"I should've guessed that you are going to be here about this time, although I thought you had given up on this place," I said, rising from the grass.

"Me, never! This is the only place that offers some amount of soberness for me. How have you been doing? I'm sorry about what has been happening to you."

"I'm all right. I guess you could say where there's life there's hope," I said. There was an elderly couple sitting in the far side of the park. My eyes caught them, making me realize that my concern about speaking with Dorothy in public, was still there. In light of what had been happening, I had grown much more conscious about that.

"Don't worry about them. I know them well, they won't tell," she said jokingly. Dorothy read my thoughts correctly.

"You are really sharp. You should do mind reading," I said seriously.

"Seeing that you have confidence in me as a mind reader, I have something else I want to say."

"Do you believe you're correct about this one?"

"Only you can answer that," she said coming a bit closer to me. "Here's a drink, if you want," she said, handing me a pop.

"Thank you."

"That picture means a lot to us. Does it mean something to you?" she asked timidly.

"What picture?"

"C'mon Luther. My mother is convinced, my Grandfather, my uncle, Joe too. It was the only picture of its kind. The other boxes disappeared from around it. That box was moved, we know that much. However, all the other pictures remain, except for that one."

I gave Dorothy all the time she wanted to speak since I needed adequate time to give her an appropriate response. "Is that enough evidence that I must have taken that picture? Grandma always told me never to take anything that doesn't belong to me. I have lived with that for most of my life," I said convincingly, reminding myself that in essence that picture belonged to me.

It belonged to me to make amends for that atrocity that was photographed on it. It was my father. Furthermore, I had every intention of returning it as soon as it served its purpose. If I was wrong on this, I earnestly asked God for forgiveness. Deep down within, I felt justified in taking it – temporarily.

Dorothy was silent. I was never good at mind reading. Somehow I had a funny feeling that Dorothy felt defeated in her attempt to solicit information from me.

"I must say I never believe for one moment that you took that picture," she said.

"You don't?" I asked, as surprised as ever.

"No, I don't. When you care about someone, that person can do no wrong in your eyes," she smiled.

"Tell me then…if I may ask, what's so important about those pictures?" I had to ask that question. Such an opportunity might not arise again. Dorothy was vulnerable at this moment as far as I was concerned. The way things had been going, it was now or never.

I had expected Dorothy to struggle with an answer. This brave girl did not have that on her mind. Maybe it was innocence, or could it be that she would have done anything to win my affection?

"The picture is dear to my family. I must admit that I don't know why."

I doubted whether she was telling the truth. "Have you ever seen it?"

"No, apparently they were taken long ago before I was born. I have seen the others…only yesterday. Mom said it's important and I take her word for it."

"What about your mother? Has she seen it?"

"I think so. My mother told me once about a terrible incident she saw when she was quite young. I want to believe that's what the picture is about."

"What incident was that?"

"I cannot say for sure. She didn't elaborate, only to say she would never forget it as long as she lived. Ma told me the lesson she had learned was to treat everyone equal, love everyone the same, and color doesn't matter."

"Hmm, that's food for thought there."

"I started to get curious after seeing what I saw happened to you. How could they do that?" she asked.

"This picture cost me my job. It must be important," I answered cautiously.

"That pig Joe! He's pushing fire. He hates your guts and wants you to go back east as soon as possible," Dorothy said angrily.

"He will have to wait a little longer."

"How much longer?"

"I don't have a deadline."

"I hope you stay as long as you want. It's rather nice to have you around here Luther," she said, reaching out for my hand. "I don't have any friends. I need a friend to talk to…share my thoughts, ideas…my love."

The first thought that hit me was to take away my hand. I didn't do that though. Dorothy squeezed my hand as hard as she could.

I found Uncle Bob, Benny and Maria waiting for me. Maria must have left school before her scheduled time.

"Ready?" she asked.

"Let me grab a sandwich," I replied.

Ol' Titus lived on the edge of town. In fact, his house was not that far from the route we used that night to visit the camp of the Ku Klux Klan.

He was a short, well-built elderly man whose hair was all white. Ol' Titus was sitting in his rocking chair, as we came up the knoll in front of his house. He lived with his wife Agatha.

"Whoa…this ain't no visit, this is an invasion, a friendly invasion," he grinned, revealing tobacco-stained teeth. "Welcome to my humble place o' abode," he said bowing gracefully.

We all acknowledge his gesture. "It's good to see you again Titus," Benny said. Benny was more familiar with him than any of us.

"Good to see you too, Ben," he grinned.

"How are you feeling now?" Uncle Bob asked.

"Ahhh! Bob, t'ank God I ain't no way worse. I've been through a rough time."

"Sometimes I was thinking he ain't gonna make it," Agatha said.

"He did. Glory be to God," I said.

"True son, very true. He deserves all the glory an' praise. You're an intelligent young man. Caleb would have been proud o' you," Agatha said.

"I have no doubt about that," Benny added.

"Ah son, yuh cause me to think…to think a lot on my sick bed. I'm an ol' man, getting so sick I could die at any time," Titus said between coughs. "Agatha and myself here have talked many times 'bout life in the past, and what is ahead for the younger ones. Slavery left us no legacy, but sorrow and pain an' we have nothing to leave fo' our children. My conscience is not clear, and I want it to be clear before God takes me home."

As I sat there listening to Ol' Titus, I started to think about my Grandmother. She must have those thoughts too.

"I knew yuh father very well…very well," he continued. We all sat in silence as if we were listening to some grand ol' storyteller. A somber look was on Uncle Bob's worried face. "He was a good man."

I wanted to say something, however, in keeping with the silence among the small audience, I decided against that.

"It was a pity he had to go in that way," Titus said. "I'm bold enough to say that I'm the oldes' man in this town. Anyone want to challenge me I'm willing to face up to it," he grinned. "I know good men when I see one. Your father was a hard working man, honest to death, innocent to death…he was a good man."

"Thanks," I mumbled softly.

"I'll always remember him. We often talk 'bout the hard times our people face. I worked at a store in town 'cross from Hay's and we often bumped into each other. The day Clinton was stabbed I'll always remember. Why? Caleb and me went to Cold Stream to have lunch. He told me how much he wanted to go to Canada to see his children and mother."

Imagine that! Was it any wonder I felt so close to Cold Stream? I was now hearing that my father visited there sometimes too – for lunch, like I did. Uncle Bob never told me that maybe because he didn't know.

On top of that, I was now learning that my father had a strong desire to return to see his children.

All the eyes in the room were on Titus. He must have felt uncomfortable for being at the center of attraction. His hands could not remain steady, a sign he could be suffering from some illness.

"A funny thing happ'n on that fateful day," Titus recalled. "'Bout half an hour after lunch, my manager sent me over to Hay's to remind him about a meeting they had planned for the following evening. When

I stepped into the store I could not understan'…it was so quiet." Titus clasped his hands to try to control the trembling. Agatha came closer to him realizing the difficulty he had keeping his hands steady.

Uncle Bob was getting uneasy in his seat. He kept shifting his position. Benny sat forward clasping his hands too. Maria, who was beside me, listened attentively as if she was under a spell.

The afternoon sun was shining brilliantly outside. Its piercing light found its way through the glass window into the living room where we were sitting. Despite the sunlight, somehow the room appeared darker to me. I must have been having a bout of dizziness or something. After all, I was hearing for the first time, a first hand account of what happened that day. I did not expect to hear this; yet the key to the puzzle was slowing turning into the keyhole.

"M-my eyes saw the blood firs'…a trail of blood leading from 'round the counter. That part of the counter was not far from the side door where I entered. I was tremblin'…"

Titus was the witness, I thought. What better witness could I have wanted, despite his silence over these many years.

"I don't like the site of blood, you know, it gives me col' shivers. I thought 'bout running back out o' the store. I saw someone… bending over Mr. Clinton Hay. There was a knife in his chest…dangling from it. His attacker started to tremble…badly when he saw me. Caleb came in from the back at the same time. Poor Caleb…he was so frightened when he saw the knife in Mr. Hay's chest. He tried to use a piece o' cloth to try to stop the bleeding."

"What did the person say to you?" I asked breaking the monologue.

"I remember clearly. I'll never forget those words. He said he would get help; I was very frightened an' told him to go on quickly.

What I was hearing with my own ears were the words of the mystery witness. I wanted to be absolutely certain about that so I had to ask the question.

"Are you the witness that the newspaper quoted?" I asked.

Titus shifted his eyes from me. I knew the answer. "The paper quoted the real attacker, not me."

"Go on Titus. This is a shock," Uncle Bob said.

Benny nodded in agreement.

"I feel very bad 'bout this. The nightmares after all these years...I-I'm sorry. I feel guilty...guilty...guilty," he said flashing his hand. I-I'm sorry I-I cannot go on... I should have been the one lynched, not Caleb. He didn't even see what happened." Titus placed his hands over his face to shield the tears but to no avail; they seeped through his fingers onto the floor.

I was touched by Titus' revelation. He had told us what we wanted to hear. He was the witness we wanted. Everyone shared his pain in telling us what actually happened that day.

Uncle Bob rose from his seat joining Agatha in consoling Titus. If it weren't for one thing, I would have told the others to let us forget about the whole thing. I know I could not do that.

Agatha went into the kitchen returning with a drink of water. Titus drank it and sat there for a while expressionless. Now was not the time to say anything, except to give comforting words.

"No one is laying blame here," I said. "As Caleb's son, all I want to know is what really happened. You have told us; you are very brave and honest for doing that. We are grateful because you have answered a lot of questions. The fact is we now know the truth."

"The truth is the most ruthless an' rebellious teenager in town at that time was the one who stabbed Mr. Hay."

Uncle Bob looked at Benny either in disbelief or disagreement over whom was the most ruthless teenager.

"Joe Tuck," they both said in unison.

My thoughts flashed to the Pearsley's. I was more leaning toward them. As far as I was concerned, they were suspects. Joe was not on my list, as I thought he would have been too young to commit such a crime.

"Yes. Joe Tuck," Titus confirmed. "Caleb told me he was in the backroom an' heard everything. Joe came into the store to demand money. Mr. Hay told him to go away. Joe turned around quickly an' stabbed him in the chest. Caleb came out the same time I came in."

I could hear a renewed vigor in Titus' voice. I was glad for that. At least, signs of guilt were nowhere in sight.

"Joe returned a few minutes later…with the Sheriff. I was standing right there when he told the Sheriff that he saw Caleb stabbing Mr. Hays."

At that moment, there was an urge in me to find Joe wherever he was and forced him to confess.

"I protested several times an' was told to shut up. I screamed an' told the Sheriff it didn't happ'n like that, but he would never listen to me. He told me if I said another word he would arres' me for interrupting his investigation. Mr. Hays was unconscious an' could not speak. Fortunately, he did not die. When he regained consciousness at the hospital, Caleb was lynched already. I could not eat or sleep for several months. I went to the Sheriffs's office several times an' he still wouldn't listen. Mr. Hays left town the following week."

"When I reached the store, he was already taken to the jail," Uncle Bob blurted out in tears. I reached across to hold his hand. Benny joined in too.

"There was nothing you could have done," I said.

"Those bastards!" Benny snarled.

"Where did Mr. Hays go? Do you know? Is he still alive?" I asked quickly.

"Folks say he went to Jackson. He could be alive. Let's hope he is…"

"Would you be willing to tell the prosecutor what you told us?" Benny asked.

"Ben, I've been waiting on this opportunity all these years to clear my conscience…to have my say. The Sheriff wouldn't listen to what I had to say. He told me he couldn't take the word of a colored man against a white man. I want my say…before I die. I want to die in peace," Titus said tearfully.

"So that was it…a cover up…no proper investigation," I said. "When the newspaper said there was a witness it was actually the criminal…Joe. The voice of the real witness was never heard."

"Yes son. Whenever he sees me he always give me that dirty look. I try to stay away from him."

"Do you think anyone else set him up to do it, or was it just a robbery," I asked, thinking about the Pearsley's.

"I don't know son. I stayed outside the jail all evening. The Sheriff wouldn't let me go in. At around ten '0' clock I decided to go home for a bite an' returned later. In fact, Bob and I both decided to do that, if I remember correctly. The Sheriff told Bob justice would be done an' there was nothing he could do. The Sheriff wouldn't even talk to me," Titus grimaced.

Uncle Bob nodded with his eyes closed. He could have been praying in his heart.

"I was very tired. After I had a bite I fell asleep. I woke up some time near dawn. Caleb's arrest was like a dream. It was the first thought that hit me. How could such a good man be locked up for a crime he never committed? I couldn't go back to sleep with that thought. I decided to go back down to the jail. My instinct told me something was wrong. About half a mile from the jail, I saw a crowd moving up Main Street. I ran towards the crowd," Titus said coughing incessantly.

Nervousness gripped my body. This could be hardest part to digest.

"I got nearer an' my worst fears were confirmed. Caleb was being dragged by an angry mob. The crowd took him up the street an' right over to Cold Stream."

"Give me strength, dear God," I said softly. Maria heard me; she held onto my hand. She had been very quiet all along.

Cold Stream was no longer a mystery. The first day I saw it, something hit home. I could not fathom it out but all I knew it gave me a feeling that was very difficult to explain. Yes, it reminded me of home. I thought that was all to it. Apparently, I was wrong.

"Caleb resisted an' it was of no use." Titus was all in tears. He had difficulty continuing. I shared his feeling. He wanted to make up for all these years to include every possible detail.

"Joe was the ringleader. The same person who was responsible for the crime was the one who hauled him up onto that horse."

"Who were the others in the crowd?" I asked.

Titus looked at Benny and Uncle Bob. "The Pearsley's…Tim Barker, Aaron Riley an' several others who have left town since. They just watched…didn't do anything. Joe and two others, who died in the war, did everything. The Sheriff came after he was already dead."

"Is the Sheriff alive?" I asked, doubting whether it could be the same one in office today.

"I don't have a clue. The last thing I heard a couple years ago was that he's retired an' living somewhere near Jackson."

"I know where he is. He lives in Glasgow, a big town a few miles from here. I learned that when I was making some checks for myself. The good news is he is now a born-again Christian," Benny said.

"Good, he may be ready to confess. Did the Ku Klux Klan have anything to do with it?" I wanted to know.

Titus looked down at his clasped hand. "I honestly don't know. They are so secretive that they could do anything."

Maria handed me the picture and I passed it on to Titus. "Do you recognize this picture?"

Titus pulled it close to his eyes examining it from corner to corner. "How could I ever forget. This is Joe," he said pointing to a man standing near the dangling body. "This could be Mr. Pearsley…and if I remember correctly, this young girl beside him is Rebecca…yes sir, Rebecca. She was there…I was hiding behind a tree not far away. Rebecca was a frightened, yet brave, child."

We all made eye contact – Maria, Benny, Uncle Joe and me. The shock on Uncle Bob's face made me want to leave. Uncle Bob looked as if he had seen a ghost.

Chapter Twelve

We returned home near dusk. Shadows of the evening were scattering across the sky. The nocturnal insects had begun their enchanting sounds. I don't know how I could sleep tonight. Uncle Joe and the others must have had those feelings too.

"We have some planning to do," Benny said. "Poor Ol Titus may be able to sleep better tonight…we can't with all of this information before us."

"Where do we start?" I asked.

Uncle Bob was not saying much. He needed time to get over the startling revelation he had heard from the mouth of Titus. Apparently, Uncle Bob had no idea that Rebecca was at the scene of the lynching.

"We have to go to Glasgow tomorrow. Saturday is a good day to do this. On Monday, we go into Jackson. There's no more time to waste," Benny said.

Sometimes I wished that kind of talk were coming from Uncle Bob. I was discovering he was absorbed into his own little world now.

"How will we get there?" Uncle Bob asked softly.

"There's a bus that goes to Glasgow. It leaves about ten every morning and returns at six."

"I'm ready," I said.

"I am too," Maria said.

"Well, I guess I'm going along," Uncle Bob said.

"We have to take the picture. Be prepared to tell Hank Kerrigan what we know," Benny said. "If he confesses we have Titus as our true witness. This means we are ready to go to Jackson," Benny said.

"I'm hoping the courts have come a long way since the 1930's. If not, we would have wasted out efforts," I said."

"Mississippi is a segregated state. There are racial problems

161

everywhere, the court being no exception. If the District Attorney won't listen we have to think of something else," Benny suggested.

Benny had a spirit I truly admired. He always had a back-up plan, should the current one backfired. As for Uncle Bob, I could see now why the investigation reached nowhere. He didn't have the commitment that was needed to make any tangible progress.

I was beginning to wonder what possible motive, if any, Rebecca had in having a relationship with my uncle. I didn't want to speculate in case I could be wrong.

"Let's sleep on it positively," I said.

"I think we should do that."

"How can I ever thank you both for what you are doing?" I told Benny and Maria at the door.

Benny smiled. "You know what son, you would have done the same for me. You get some sleep now."

Maria squeezed my hand. They disappeared into the darkness leaving me to wish they had stayed a little longer. What we had accomplished this afternoon was too precious not to have a celebration.

Glasgow was a nice little town. The journey there was under two hours. The bus made a few stops to pick up as well as drop off passengers. By midday, we cruised into the town's center.

We hopped off and headed for Blake Street, where Hank lived. Benny knew where he was going, making it easier for us.

It took us fifteen minutes to reach number 37. We walked right up into a small driveway that led to the verandah. Cautiously, we knocked on the door three times. There was no answer. We knocked again, still no answer.

I hated to think we had traveled so far to come out here only to be met with disappointment. I stepped passed Benny and knocked again, this time much louder. There were footsteps inside the house.

Suddenly, the door was half opened. An elderly white lady peered through the slot at me.

"What do you want?" she asked, rather slowly.

"We are here to see Mr. Hank Kerrigan," I said politely.

"What business do you have with him?" the woman said. She was about to close the door.

"Please ma'am…we came all the way here to see him. Can you tell us where we can find him? This is very, very important," I said, putting out a little urgency in my voice.

"What do you want to see him for?" the lady asked.

Benny stepped forward. "It concerns a hanging ma'am. This young man's father was lynched many years ago. All he wants to do is ask Mr. Kerrigan a few questions."

The lady looked at us up from head to toe. She examined each face closely before she decided to open the door partially. "You better thank sweet Jesus that he's born again. Wait here," she said, closing the door on us.

In less than a minute, the door opened again and Hank stood there. Hank's hair was all white, although he didn't look that old. His bulging stomach might have made him appear older. He was a short man with a very plump body. He could not have had on all that weight during his sojourn as Sheriff. Undoubtedly, he would have trouble running or even walking fast.

"What can I do for you gentlemen?" he asked coming out on the verandah to join us. "Ohhh," he said, looking at Uncle Bob and Benny. "I remember those faces."

The woman, who must be his wife, was still looking at us suspiciously.

"About twenty years ago, Caleb Nesbeth was lynched while you were the Sheriff in Clarksville. I need to know how come an innocent man was lynched. That man was my father."

Hank sat down in a chair nearby, a creaking sound burst out as soon as he lowered his full weight into it. From all indications, he was ready to talk. With arms folded, I was ready to listen. The others were waiting, too.

"First I must say, I have nothing to hide. I'm now born-again, Praise the Lord. Whatever wrongs were done in the past…that was what they were, in the past. The good Lord forgives," he replied, showing no emotions.

Hank's coldness and indifference to what I just told him surprised me. . This visit could be a blessing in disguise though.

"Initially, I thought your father was guilty. Certainly, he didn't deserve to die…not in that way. No human being deserves to die that way for that matter. No one should take the law into their own hands. It was wrong, too, in that the crime didn't fit the punishment. But what makes you think he was innocent?"

Benny indicated to me with a nod to go ahead and respond to Hank's question. At first, I thought he wanted to do that after I saw his lips parted to say something. "I'm curious to know why you didn't listen to what my father had to say about the incident?"

"I did listen…only…" Hank answered.

"I don't think you did. If you did he wouldn't have been arrested," I said forcefully.

"How come? What is it that you know that I don't."

"That the same man you listened to is the same man who committed the crime. The only witness was right there, somehow you wouldn't even listen to him. The words of a white man are worth more than that of a colored man. In fact, a colored man has no say in matters of justice…even when his life is at stake."

"Joe Tuck…" Hank mumbled, hanging his head as if embarrassed. "I wanted to stop the lynching…the mob was too angry for me. They wouldn't listen to me."

"Did you ever speak with Mr. Hay?" I asked.

"Yes, I did speak with him."

"What did he say?"

Hank, aware that his wife was nearby, bit his lip. Would a born again Christian lie before so many witnesses? I hardly thought so.

"He confessed that…that Joe did it…" Hank stopped there uncertain whether to continue. Tears stream down his face.

"It wasn't too late then," I said. "There was a chance to clear his name. Why didn't you do it?"

Uncle Bob wanted to say something. "You told Ben and me that everything would be fine. The next thing I know my brother was dead.

And even after his death you knew the truth…you did nothing about it! I can't believe this! We came to your office a few times. I remember one time you told us to get out of your office. Do you remember that?"

Hank nodded. "I remember everything. How could I ever forget that, the most painful day of my career? If I weren't a Christian I would have so much guilt. Thank God my conscience is now free. I have confessed and repented before God."

"My father won't come back in this life. However, his name is tainted. He's a criminal in the eyes of Clarkesville. We are here to find out what you can do for us," I said putting him on the spot. "We want to clear his name, nothing more, nothing less."

"Do what is right," Hank's wife said surprisingly.

"What do you want me to do?" he asked.

"We are going to Jackson on Monday, to speak with the District Attorney. We need something from you…a written statement or your presence…whatever will be needed."

"Do it Hank! God is watching. This young man seems to be serious in wanting to clear his father's name. Do the right thing," his wife said, coming to stand beside him.

"I'll write a statement. If that's not enough I'll do whatever they want me to do. Your father didn't deserve that," Hank said solemnly.

"Thank you Jesus," I blurted out without even thinking of it.

"Is there anything else you can tell us?" Benny asked.

"I better get busy with this letter. It will have everything. If that's not enough, I'm willing to appear in person." he suggested.

"I truly appreciate your help suh," I told him.

"Although I'm retired, it's my duty. I owe you this, I owe it in the name of justice."

"You could have refused. There's such a racial hatred in this country that some would have dismissed us long ago because it's a colored man that is involved. We thank you very much for accommodating us suh," I replied.

"You are a very polite young man. Have you been living here all the time?"

"No sir, I live in Canada with my Grandmother."

He was taken aback by my answer.

"You mean you came all the way here to prove your father's innocence?" he asked in disbelief.

"Yes suh. This is something I pledged to do when I learned he was lynched."

"Son, I commend you for your resilience and commitment to this cause. Many people, both colored and white, have been lynched without getting a fair trial. Unfortunately, most of them have been coloreds. After hearing this from you, I am more than happy to do this for you," Hank said, the expression on his face leaning toward a smile.

We all were smiling. We had every reason with this day turning out to be a very productive one. Indeed, it could turn out to be the most productive. We have the testimony of a former lawman – not any ordinary lawman, but rather the one that arrested my father.

On Sunday morning, we got dressed early for church. There was a lot to be thankful for. With all that had happened in the past few days, I could return to Canada soon. I started to feel happy about that prospect.

Maria greeted me at the door of the church. Since our trip to Glasgow, Maria had been wearing a permanent smile. Imagine- it was not her father yet she showed so much concern about my case; it was unbelievable.

Mostly everyone was seated in the church minutes before the service was about to begin. I noticed some people were looking toward the door. There was silence; the organ that was playing stopped suddenly.

Two figures walked into the church. Rebecca and Dorothy came right up to the front row. This must have been the first time they ever visited this church. So near, yet they were so far away.

The pastor started the service as soon as they were seated. The service was not anything out of the ordinary.

Both women tried to blend in with the crowd as best as they could. When it was all over, Dorothy had no problem picking me out of the crowd. I saw Uncle Bob walking up to Rebecca.

"This is one helluva service," Dorothy said laughing. "Oh, I shouldn't use that word. I should say that was one heavenly service."

"Glad you like it. Tell me, is it the first time you are coming here?" I asked.

"As a matter of fact, yes. I'm so ashamed to say that. We live here all these years and it is the first time I am attending service in this church."

"That is understandable. It's a colored church."

"You know that doesn't mean a thing to us," she said grim faced.

"What made you change your mind?"

"That's a long story. Let's go outside," she said, leading the way.

I didn't see Maria. She must have disappeared somewhere when Dorothy came up to me.

"Hank Kerrigan called my mother last night. After he spoke with her, she couldn't stop crying. I guess I don't have to say who Hank is because you were there yesterday."

'That's correct. You look lovely today."

Dorothy's hair was shining in the sunlight. A slight wind was blowing; at times it blew a part of her hair into her face.

"Thank you. If I can remember, it's the first compliment I have ever received from you. Hmm, things are changing around here, wouldn't you agree?"

"You should know. Why did Hank call your mother?" I asked, watching her reaction closely.

"To tell her that your uncle was lynched innocently."

"My father," I corrected her unintentionally. It was too late; I had spilled the beans. Hank didn't mention that part of it.

Dorothy's mouth was wide open. "Your father? Caleb was your father...how come..."

"...I didn't say it," I said, finishing her sentence. "I came here from Canada to learn the truth about his death. Understandably, I couldn't say anything."

A tear rolled down her cheek. "I'm sorry. I'm sorry..."

"All I want to know is why he was lynched without a proper trial."

"Mom told me everything last night. An angry mob, my Grandfather and granduncle were there too.

That was it. Hank didn't mention the Pearsley's, however, the fact

167

that he called Rebecca last night was an indication that they could have been involved somehow.

"Your mother was there too…at the lynching?" I asked.

"Yes, she told me that to this day she cannot get it out of her mind. That's why she's so close to Uncle Bob. She feels obligated to him."

"How close?"

Dorothy turned away her head to look at me. "Let's say as close as can be."

"Whatever that means?"

"Tell me, what do you intend to do now?" she asked in a tone that suggested that she wanted a clear answer.

"I want to clear my father's name. I also want the perpetrators brought to justice."

"That will be very difficult to prove. It's been so long."

"The most important thing is to clear his name. If that's achieved, I don't believe it will be that difficult to find the culprits. Furthermore, the victim is alive and he did make a confession," I said confidently. I could see the interest on her face.

"Huh, you have been doing a lot of work Luther. Where did you get time to do all this?"

"Remember I'm no longer working," I laughed.

Uncle Bob and Rebecca walked up to where we were standing. "Luther, you are on interesting young man. You had to be Caleb's son," Rebecca said.

"You knew my father that well?"

"I was a teenager when he died. The little I learned about him was from your uncle and a few folks around here. I am sorry Luther. He should never have died that way."

"Hank spoke with her Luther. I had to tell her about you," Uncle Bob said.

"Dorothy told me he called."

"Where do you go from here?" Rebecca asked.

"My first mission is to clear his name. What comes after is left to be seen." I didn't want to elaborate on the latter statement too much. In the long run, some people could get themselves involved criminally.

"I think he deserves that. I saw what happened; how could I forget? A human being, no matter what color or creed, should never have been killed like that," she said.

If I had the nerve, I would have wanted to know who instigated that mob violence. "This town owes us an apology."

"I couldn't agree more," Rebecca said.

"That will have to come soon," Dorothy said.

We bade goodbye, and joined Benny and Maria who were waiting and then head for home.

There was a pathway leading to the main road that was quicker than going through the main gate. I was the one who saw him first – a few yards away from the main entrance. He was standing on the other side of the road. There was no second guessing about who he was waiting for.

The others were chatting away, unaware of his presence. It was not until we were only a few feet away that Maria raised the alarm.

"Look who is here," she whispered.

"Hmm, I smell trouble," Benny said.

"Even at the church he wants to start trouble," Uncle Bob chuckled.

We walked on pretending we didn't see him.

Joe Tuck watched us carefully, holding his ground.

"Hey boy…you Canadian boy, I'm talking to you."

Hank Kerrigan must have had a busy night informing all the relevant parties about my presence and my intentions.

Typical of my past experiences with Mighty Joe, I said nothing.

"You scum! Don't pull this one on me again. I'm talking to you…lay off!" he said walking toward me.

Benny stopped in his tracks. "Make one step further and you will regret it," he challenged him.

"Who the hell do you think you are boy?" he snarled at Benny. "Who told you to open your mouth? Did I ask your opinion?" he asked, clenching his fist.

"You must be the deaf one. One step closer…as I told you before, you will regret it," Benny said boldly. For a man of his age, Benny was no coward. I proved that again today, recalling what happened when

Joe visited our house the other night. Me, I had no such guts.

Joe stood firm. I was expecting him to come forward charging like a bull but instead, he retreated.

"The wrath of the Lord Jesus Christ is on you Joe Tuck. Your days are numbered," Benny said. "I wouldn't waste time laying a hand on you."

Suddenly, Joe turned and walked away. Behind us Rebecca and Dorothy were walking through the gate. Joe must have seen them and hurriedly made his way through another pathway leading to the adjoining the street. We burst out laughing. There was no way Joe could not have heard us.

We followed Benny and Maria home after they invited us for Sunday dinner. In a sense, it was a kind of celebration too. We had our fill eventually getting into a conversation about our progress so far. We also discussed where we intend to go from here with the information we had.

"I have a little doubt in my mind that Hank is going to back down in some of the things he said," I declared to all three of them.

"Well, we have the confession with us. It's a pity we cannot open it to see what's inside," Benny said.

"It's sealed and addressed to Abe Winters, District Attorney, Jackson, MS. There is nothing we can do about it. Let's hope he honors his commitment. If he's called on in court, let's hope, too, he cooperates fully," I said.

"I believe he will," Maria said. "If he's a true born again Christian, he will."

"You have a good point there," Uncle Bob said. "I was surprised he called Rebecca."

"Did Rebecca say why?" I asked.

"Yes. She told me Hank wanted to inform them that my father was an innocent man. He told her Mr. Hays had confessed to him but he had never disclosed that to anyone."

"What about Joe? I would imagine Joe now knows that he's in big, big trouble," I said with a smile. At last, I felt a touch of sweet revenge although this was not about revenge. In the case of Joe, I simply wanted him to come down from that high chair he had been sitting on all these years.

"That's why he came all the way to the church to try to scare you. He couldn't wait," Benny said.

"Vengeance is mine, saith the Lord. He'll have to answer to man and to God," Uncle Bob said.

"I can hardly wait to hear what the District Attorney will say about all this evidence," I said.

"We have the picture, although that doesn't prove anything. We have Ol' Titus, who witnessed the stabbing and the lynching. And we have the word of the sheriff who was the arresting officer. What would be good is to find Mr. Hays himself. He is also in Jackson," Benny said.

"You know I wasn't even thinking about that? That's so true. We may have to spend an extra day there. This gives me an idea," I said scratching my head. "Let's try to find Mr. Hays first before going to the District Attorney

Everybody's face lit up with a smile. Maria leaned over to whisper something in my ear. "That's why I love you so much,' she whispered. The others heard and laughed aloud. Jackson, here we come.

Chapter Thirteen

Jackson was a huge, cosmopolitan city. A thick cluster of brick structures greeted us when we came off the bus at the terminal. The city was heavily populated with both people and buildings.

The first thing on our agenda was to find a bite to eat. Benny warned us that we just couldn't go into any place to eat in Jackson. I had noticed one place with a "Whites Only," sign but it never occurred to me that it truly meant that. Indeed, I had to remind myself that this is a segregated part of the country.

To my surprise, we found a small restaurant where only colored people were eating. It was rather strange at first, taking me a few minutes for it to register in my brain that I would not be seeing any white people in there. It was a restaurant catering specifically to coloreds.

"Maybe here would be a good place to start asking some questions," I said to the others.

Benny agreed. "That's a good idea." Benny got up to walk over to the cashier. I could hear him asking a question; the cashier nodded with a bow. She pointed through the door.

"Never heard of Clinton Hays," Benny said. "She told me about a store up the road where the owner might know him.

Anxious to learn more, we left the restaurant for the store. A pot-bellied man, his lower abdomen resting against the counter, rolled his eyes at us when we entered.

"What do you want?" he asked gruffly.

"Do you know a gentleman by the name of Clinton Hays?" I asked.

The man examined me thoroughly, as if to say 'who are you?' "What do you want with him?" he asked, his eyes studying my face.

"We need to talk with him. It's very important suh," I answered.

"Four coloreds wanting to see a man must be very important," he said. "I never heard of any such man. Try King Street on the other side. If he's a businessman, he'll be there."

The walk over to King Street took us five minutes. It was crowded with traffic. This must be one of, if not the busiest street in the city. We didn't know where to begin.

Maria pointed to a shoe store where King crossed with another street. We decided to try that one. Maria volunteered to go it alone given our experience with the previous visit.

We watched her waltzed toward the store, her hips swaying up and down. She was dressed sharply with matching colors.

Maria emerged about a minute later. Unfortunately, the person had never heard of Mr. Hays. He, too, suggested we checked other stores up the street. We took the advice at heart checking eight more stores. They were all the same – none of them had ever heard of Mr. Hays.

By the time we finished the tenth store on our walk, we were totally exhausted and frustrated.

"What do we do now?" Uncle Bob asked.

I could see the weariness and disappointment in his face. "Mr. Hays must be somewhere around. We have to find him, it's our last hope," I said.

"We'll have to stay overnight. The trouble is where do we go to find somewhere to cater to us," Benny said.

"Let's go back to the restaurant. That seems to be the only place we know for now," I said.

"Let's go," a tired-sounding Maria said. She held onto my hand for support some of the time. I thought about that too. Was it for comfort, or something else?

We found the restaurant without any problem. The cashier, who we had seen near lunchtime, was not there. An older woman was occupying that seat.

We ordered some coffee. "Have you ever heard of a Mr. Clinton Hays who may own some business here in Jackson?" I asked the cashier at the same time I was paying for the coffee.

The woman took up the money. I could hear her repeating the name under her breath.

"Clinton Hays…Hays…Hays. Why does that name soun' so familiar?" she asked.

That gave me a little hope.

"A colored man or a white man?" she asked.

"White," I answered.

"I have been doing business here too long not to know him. There ain't no businessman in this town that I don't know young man. Grew up here all my life. Hmm, funny? Clinton Hays? I should know him."

"I would be grateful ma'am. I need to talk to him very badly."

"What he got for yuh?"

"Nothing really. He may have some very important information I need to know," I replied.

"Oh, I see one o' them lawyer types," she laughed, exposing perfect teeth.

"You could say that," I said quickly, not paying any attention to her compliment, but rather anxious for her to put a face to the name. I had on nice clothes, my Sunday best, however, not for a moment did I ever had any reason to believe I could be passed for a young colored lawyer. Benny had emphasized before our departure that we should dress properly if we were going to seek information. His idea was paying off now.

"Yuh know what, yuh look to be a very bright young man and you express yuhself very well. Put on your best," she said, referring to my speech, "leave your others behind and go to the store right at the corner from here. You will see Mr. Hart, tell him I sent you…Louise Brinkley, and tell him you need to contact Mr…the man you need. If Mr. Hart doesn't know, then no one is in Jackson by that name. Yes suh, I guarantee you that," she grinned at me.

"I sure thank you for that ma'am. You give me some hope here. Thanks again," I smiled at her. I told the others and we left together.

It was not until I was in front of the store that I realized that it was the same one we had gone to first. My heart sank in disbelief. Anyway, I told the others to wait for me outside

Mr. Hart stopped what he was doing as soon as I walked in. Fortunately, he didn't appear too busy giving him hardly any excuse for not wanting to see me. .

"What can I do for you now? Alone this time eh?" he asked.

He had a sharp memory. For someone who saw dozens of faces each day, one would have thought that he wouldn't remember me.

"Louise Brinkley says you can help," I said softly.

"Oh, Louise sent you? Ah! Why didn't you say that in the first place?" he smiled.

"Because she didn't. We had spoken with someone else," I told him.

"Hmm, so is it the same question…Clinton Hays?"

"Yes suh."

"I know him," he admitted readily, frowning in his process. "He has a small furniture shop north of here. You take King Street, go north to Main, turn left onto Park Avenue. His shop is about a block down. You will see the sign 'Clinton's Furniture Store.' He is a fine gentleman. Is he in any trouble?" Mr. Hart asked.

"No, not at all. He will give more help than we could ever imagine."

"Tell him I send my regards."

"Thank you suh. I do appreciate your help," I replied, meaning every word I had said.

The others didn't believe that I had finally found Mr. Hay. They all looked at me like I was speaking a different language. I kept rehearsing his address in my head and just spilled it out at them. Without any hesitation, they accepted my claim.

Mr. Hays was really on the other side of town. It took us thirty-five minutes to get there. The store stood right before us its sign glaring at us in big and bold letters.

As we entered the door, Mr. Hays recognized Benny. My heartbeat accelerated faster.

"Don't I know you from somewhere?" he asked.

"Clarkesville," Benny said.

"C-Clarkesville," he said slowly. I could see memories coming back for him. His face was serious for a brief time. Then he smiled soberly.

"Nice town although I vowed never to return there," he said scornfully.

"Because of your experience," Benny stated.

"You know…you should know. Dear God, what an experience," Mr. Hays said, looking up into the ceiling.

"That's why we are here," Benny said.

Mr. Hays turned his attention to all of us, examining each one of us with some amount of consternation. "Interesting faces," he muttered under his breath.

I watched him closely, scrutinizing the expression on his face to the way his blue eyes surveyed our presence. Aging had been kind to Mr. Hays. The gray hairs were more generous because he did not seem an elderly man. Seemingly, he had taken care of himself, despite his near death experience. From all indications he had recovered superbly well.

"This young man," Benny said pointing to me, "is the son of the man who was lynched innocently following your attack," Benny said politely. We came here to get your side of the story. He traveled all the way from Canada to clear his father's name. That's the least we can do now."

"Sweet Lord, how great thou art…thank you for this moment of my life," Mr. Hays said both trembling hands rubbing his balding head. Mr. Hays could be nearing his God-given figure of seventy. A few grays were sticking out of his ears and nose, as well as the thin patch of hair on his receding hairline. He was thinly built with the veins in his hands were swelling out of the skin.

"Are you going back to Clarkesville tonight?" he asked. "I need some time to talk with all of you."

"As a matter of fact, we don't have much time here. We have to find somewhere to stay tonight," Uncle Bob said.

"Good," Mr. Hays said with a handclap. "Which one of you is Luther's brother? I know he had one," he said, rubbing both hands together.

"That's me," Uncle Bob told him.

"I've rooms to spare. My wife died a few years ago, may God bless her soul. I've been alone. I wouldn't mind some company for supper. I owe that to you," Mr. Hays said, almost pleading.

We had a good supper at Mr. Hays' small house about ten minutes from Park Avenue. He was well organized. Supper came in no time. We had been too busy the entire afternoon, never realizing the extent of our hunger until the food was set before us.

After supper, we told Mr. Hays about Mr. Kerrigan's decision to assist us. We thought that would it easier for Mr. Hays to do likewise.

"Joe Tuck wanted money to bribe people to finance his organization," Mr. Hays told us around the supper table.

"The Ku Klux Klan," I said.

"How did you know that? Hmm, Joe's father was the one who started the organization in Clarkesville. After he died, Joe took over and never looked back."

"It has become his life," I replied.

"He wanted me to support the Klan and I refused. He thought the easiest way of getting my money was to steal it. Although he was a teenager, he was very strong. He tried to place the knife at my throat. I tried to wrestle myself free from his grip. He overpowered me stabbing me right here," he explained, pointing to the spot on his right side. Someone came in the store to see him standing over me."

"Do you know Titus?" Benny asked.

"No," he replied.

"He came in that time. Caleb came from the back afterwards and was trying to stop your bleeding. Joe had told them he was going for help."

"Yes, he went for the sheriff instead," Mr. Hays said. "When the sheriff came I was unconscious…couldn't speak. The shock of my life came after I learned poor Caleb was lynched for stabbing me. The very man that tried to help me was accused falsely. I told the sheriff, who never acted on it. That was why I had to leave Clarkesville. Joe Tuck threatened me constantly that if spoke the truth I would be a dead meat."

"Would you be willing to tell the court that?" I asked.

"If it means clearing his name, yes," Mr. Hays said sadly.

"Did the Pearsley's have anything to do with the lynching that you know of?" I asked.

There was utter silence. I had to ask that question though. Now was the time to do that regardless of what Uncle Bob might think.

"I honestly don't know. A mob was responsible for the lynching. It would be very difficult in a court of law to prove they had a direct role, if that was the case. To separate onlookers from those directly responsible could be difficult," Mr. Hays said.

I handed him the picture.

"Where did you get this?" he asked, looking from the picture to me

"I found it in the basement of the Pearsley's old home."

He peered at the picture. "That is Alfred there…that must be his daughter Rebecca. They were there, however, does that mean they were involved? That's a question for the prosecutors."

"What do you think will happen to Joe Tuck? Benny asked.

"The case is nearly twenty years old. I don't know. I believe the important thing is clearing Caleb's name."

"That's right," I said, trying to determine what uncle Bob was thinking. Was he angry with me?

"Tomorrow, we'll go to the District Attorney to present our case," Benny added.

Mr. Hays was a rather hospitable man. After our little conversation, he brought out the drinks. We did have a few being careful not to overdo it. Alcohol was hard to get these days, a very precious commodity.

The next morning after breakfast we walked into town. On our way, we saw a huge puff of smoke coming from one of the buildings on the same street we were walking. Soon enough, several people started to walk in that direction.

The red glow of fire coupled with the choking smell of smoke was right before us. The building was surrounded with fire engines and shouts for water. There wasn't much the crowd could do; the heat and smoke were deterrents to any kind of help that was intended. The task proved formidable to the firemen much more amateurs like us.

A young man came up beside me, notepad in hand, writing away like crazy. "Do you work in the building?" he asked, writing at the same time as he was speaking.

"No, are you a reporter or something?"

"Yes. I work for the Jackson Post," he said, still writing.

"I have a bigger story than this, if you are interested," I said, taking a chance with what I had in mind. I never thought of it before. Something must have spurred me to make that suggestion.

Maria nudged me with her elbow. Both Uncle Bob and Benny, who heard the question, were about to say something. They changed their mind allowing me to continue to talk with the reporter. Mr. Hays was too busy with some friendly folks nearby discussing all possible causes for the fire.

"What did you say...a bigger story?" he asked.

"I'm not a reporter...huh I think it would make one heck of a story. It could grace the front page of...The Jackson Post," I said confidently.

"Well, what is it? You better be good because this fire is getting bigger and hotter," he said, putting his hand over his forehead to escape the heat.

"Sheriff's Cover Up Led to Lynching." I said waiting for his reaction. The reporter put his pen to his mouth halting whatever he was about to write.

"Is this a joke," he asked.

"No. I'm giving you the headline first," I remarked.

"Give me the body, you let the editor decide the headline," he suggested. "Go on...I hope the body will explain the headline."

"My father was lynched nearly twenty years ago for attempted murder. He was never tried instead he was taken out of jail by a mob and lynched. The guilty person, a white man, was the one who organized the lynching. Today, the culprit walks free... Is this going to make the front page?"

The reporter's face lit up. "Hmm, you have something there. Unfortunately, that's only a theory; what about the evidence? That happened twenty years ago."

"How about this? I have confessions from the sheriff himself...a born again Christian," I said, showing him the sealed envelop from my bag, "I have a picture of the lynching, most importantly, an eye witness to the crime. The victim of the crime has also confessed. He was stabbed but lived to tell the truth about what happened. He's right here in

Jackson. Twenty years ago, the sheriff of Clarkesville, Mississippi, was told the truth about the innocence of Caleb Nesbeth. That didn't seem to matter. He allowed my father to be lynched."

The reporter listened attentively knocking his pen against his chin. He fell into a reflective mood. A question was coming that at first I thought I would not be able to answer.

"Can you bring me the confession of the victim by tomorrow. If you do, then we have something big here. Nothing much is happening in Jackson these days. This is bound to make the headlines. Even if my editor doesn't like the tone, he would have to bite his tongue and run this one," he said.

I pointed to Mr. Hays standing two feet away. "That gentleman Is Mr. Hays...he was the victim," I said simply.

Mr. Hays turned around at the mention of his name. "What can I do for the gentleman?" he asked.

"This is a reporter for The Jackson Post. He is interested in our story," I told him.

"Whoa...you are interested? Who wouldn't be? After twenty years, I'm ready to talk. Let us go somewhere to talk,' Mr. Hays suggested.

We left the fire for a nearby park. Uncle Bob provided the details leading up to the arrest and Mr. Hays filled in the other details.

"We were heading for the District Attorney before we met," I told him.

The reporter laughed. "When he sees the headline tomorrow morning I guarantee you this will push him faster to open this case. I guess your motive is to clear your father's name."

"Exactly," I said.

The District Attorney wasn't amused when we met him the next morning. Mr. Hays had insisted that we stay another night and go to the District Attorney after the story had been published.

Abe Winters was furious that the former Sheriff knew all along and made no effort to at least clear my father's name.

"How could he?" he shouted. "We have been trying to discourage lynching for years because even a toddler can see there is no justice in them. By keeping silence, we are indirectly supporting them," he echoed vociferously.

We sat in his office listening to him to do all the talking. A sense of relief was coming over me slowly as I saw my mission coming to an end.

"We will proceed to open this case right away. The evidence is overwhelming. What more can I say gentlemen. To you in particular Mr. Nesbeth, we are going to get to the bottom of this case. We aim to fix it…I can assure we will do our best to have your father's name cleared."

"Thank you suh. My father deserves this. Believe me, he does."

"No doubt he does. I'm happy Mr. Hays lives here and is with us. He's key to the whole case. I will be calling Mr. Kerrigan later today, to ensure we have no further delay in getting this trial going once and for all."

We left Jackson a relieved bunch, having put in place all the ingredients to re-open the case. Mission accomplished. On arrival in Clarkesville, on Thursday afternoon, we went to Ol' Titus to tell him what had transpired in Jackson. He was quite emotional about the news vowing to tell the truth and nothing but the truth, "So help me God."

On our way back, we stopped at Rebecca. The two Pearsley's and Dorothy were behind the counter when we came in. They were discussing an interesting subject, judging from the look on their faces. Immediately, their faces became grim and perplexed, as our presence captured their attention.

"Your picture is in the hands of the District Attorney in Jackson," I said. "I have asked him to return it to you if he doesn't need it."

They all stared at me speechless. "We're sorry," Jacob said, as if he had expected me to say what I had just told them. "There comes a time in our lives when we have to admit mistakes. We have to try to correct what was wrong. We want to say unequivocally that we took no part in that lynching. We were only spectators. Yes, probably we could and should have done something to stop it. We never did. That was our mistake, not ours only, the whole citizenry of Clarkesville." Mr. Pearsley said.

"We're sorry Luther," Rebecca interjected.

"Joe Tuck has just been arrested by the sheriff. Your father's name will be cleared," Dorothy added.

"I want to say thank you too," I told them. "You have supported my uncle all these years. You did that for me, too, during my short time here. For that, I want to say thank you very much. Now, I must go, not returning empty-handed. I'm going with the knowledge that soon, very soon, my dead father's name will once and for all be cleared."

They came over to shake my hand. Dorothy came over and gave me a hug right before everybody. "Please come back," she whispered in my ear.

Outside the store, Uncle Bob, Benny and Maria were taken aback that I was leaving before the trial. "You will understand that Grandma and Kate need me. I have been here too long now. As soon as the trial is ready, which may not be for another six months, I'll be back...with Grandma," I told them.

Uncle Bob laughed aloud, something he had not done in a while. "I would appreciate that son. I haven't seen my mother in a very long time."

Maria was on the verge of crying. She came and hugged me too. "We understand that you have to go. The good thing is you are planning to return."

"I'll return. I want to sit on that bench to hear with my own ears that Caleb Nesbeth was innocent of the crime he was lynched for."

"All of us wish for that," Benny said.

"I couldn't have done this without the support of all of you," I said.

"In this case, four heads were better than one," Maria said.

Early next morning, I boarded a bus for Louisville, Kentucky, the first of three buses I would use to return to Bakersfield. I came to the United States in secret; this time I was returning in the open.

Maria was at the terminus to see me off, along with the others. Unbeknownst to me, they had brought several gifts to take back, something I had forgotten about. We all embraced each other. For Maria it was a long and personal one.

"Remember Luther Nesbeth that I love you, and will always wait for you," she said between small sobs.

"You are a wonderful woman," I said. "You take good care of yourself. I'll write soon. Please remember I'll be back." That was all I could say.

The next five minutes found me on a bus speeding away from Clarkesville, with a mind saturated with my experiences of the past few months. Already, I was cherishing the memories and thriving on the dreams ahead. I had a lot to think about on the journey.

Bakersfield came near midday on Sunday. It was the same small town; nothing much had changed.

I walked up the pathway to the house trying desperately to carry the luggage I had. Fortunately, I took the bus passing near to our house meaning I did not have to worry about that aspect of the journey.

Grandma and Kate would have been back from service by now. And I was right. As I was walking up the house, she came out of the house in time to lay eyes on me.

"My good Lord! Look who's here…Kate! Kate! Look who is here," she yelled. "Good Lord, yuh have taken him back safe an' soun'. Thank you Jesus."

Grandma rushed towards me. I saw Kate coming too. I dropped the bags immediately to allow for one big embrace. We held each other for a while, crying and laughing at the same time.

Later inside the house, I filled them in on everything, mainly my desire to take them both to the trial.

"That would be my reward in this life," Grandma said. "I'll also get to see Bob. Son, with God all things are possible."

"Did you like it there?" Kate asked.

"It is not a bad place. It was very lonely at times I have to admit. I kept wondering if everything was okay up here. Where's Lena? I should go over there now," I said.

Grandma and Kate said nothing about that. "Is something wrong?" I asked.

Kate looked at Grandma. "Lena went to live in Halifax, Nova Scotia, three months ago. She found a job over there. We haven't heard from her since," she said sadly.

My blood ran cold. Admittedly, I missed her terribly. I was looking forward to seeing her but now, she was not around. I had been depending on her to help take care of Grandma. I was utterly disappointed.

"I know that's going to hurt," Kate said. "Lena missed you badly…in fact she was hurt. I believe that's her way of saying she couldn't wait on you," she said holding onto my hand.

"I understand. I perfectly understand. Maria will be glad to hear this."

"Who's Maria?" Grandma asked.

"A wonderful girl I met in Clarkesville. The last thing she told me at the bus terminal was that she would be waiting on me…if things didn't work out with Lena."

Grandma and Kate burst out in laughter. I left them there laughing and walked down to my favorite place, my little stream. There, it stood, flowing as it usually did – so calm, so relaxing. I felt at home again.

Five months later, we all went to the trial in Jackson. It lasted for two weeks. Everyone I knew in Clarkesville turned out. In addition, there were scores of people I didn't know.

Jacob and A.T. Pearsley were questioned but no charge was laid against them. The judge ruled that there was not enough evidence to support claims by Joe Tuck that they encouraged him to do the lynching. The judge said Joe's sole motive was to cover his tracks because he was guilty of the charge of attempted murder. He pointed to the inadequacies of prosecuting any one person for the lynching.

I had my reservation about the Pearsley's involvement. The way they reacted to the picture I had taken gave me reason to believe that they had been hiding something. However, the important thing was my father's name. God would avenge all evil that was done in the dark.

Ol' Titus did a marvelous job of being a true witness. I could see that a big burden had been taken off his shoulder. He told the judge he could now die in peace. Apparently, the judge was very moved by his testimony. Mr. Hays did equally well, and his testimony drove the final nail into the coffin of Mighty Joe. Grandma, Kate and I stood proudly and listened as the judge ruled, on the advise of the jury, that Joe Tuck was guilty of attempted murder. Caleb Nesbeth was an innocent victim of the horror of lynching. That was what truly mattered.

We hugged, cried, danced and screamed to show our delight. Mark Blair, the reporter who broke the story came over and shook my hand. His photographer took a picture of all of us.

"This picture will run above the one of the lynching to show comparison," he said.

"That's fine with us," I said. "I can hardly wait to see the headline."

"This story will go all around the country," he said. "It's not everyday we get a story like this."

I had one thing to do before I left this courthouse. I saw Joe Tuck was about to be led away. I walked over to him quickly.

Joe's face was red with anger. "You!..." he barked at me, at a loss for words.

"I can't forget that night, when a bottle was thrown. It had to be you. That was when the trouble started with you and me. Are you going to get your brothers to get you out?" I teased. "I can hardly believe I have lived to see this day to see this scum...the dregs of the earth be put away for ten years. If I were the judge I would have thrown away the key! " I told him.

A policeman held onto Joe's harm dragging him away without giving him the opportunity to say another word. Mighty Joe Tuck has had his day – finally.

There were cheers behind me. I turned to see Rebecca and Dorothy, Maria, Benny, Ol' Titus, Uncle Bob, Kate, Grandma, and Mr. Hays clapping.

The first order of business in Clarkesville, was to visit my father's grave. Each of us took a flower and placed it on it. I could see the relief on Grandma's face when she said: "my son, yuh is innocent as the day yuh was born. In death, too, yuh is innocent my child. Praise the Lord."

"We all did it for you and one day soon we will reunite. Thank you Jesus," I said.

"I never knew you. I'm happy to stand right here beside you now Dad," I said, bursting into tears. We all came close forming a semi circle hold each other's hand and said Psalm 23.

After we paid our last respects, Maria and I separated from the crowd. I told her about Lena's departure and she answered with a kiss. I told her she could come back to Canada with me to get married and again she answered with a another kiss.

There was one thing I had to do before my departure. I could not go without doing it. I held Maria's hand as we walked into town. I remembered clearly the first day I took the journey to Cold Stream. It flowed back to me again and I greeted the memories with a smile.

Cold Stream flowed like on any other day I had been there, but today I watched its ripples and listened to its trickle, comparing it to the one back home in Canada. Somehow, deep into my psyche I discerned a common factor; there was something mysterious about them. A mystery that would continue to be just that – a mystery. I could not tell, neither could I explain this close attachment, unless it had something to do with the beginning of a life, meaning where I was born, and the end of a life, where my father's journey on this planet came to a disgraceful end.

"This was where my father was lynched," I said. "I decided I wouldn't take Grandma and Kate here. It would be too much for them. For me, it's significant."

"I agree. This is one place that you'll never forget," Maria said, clutching my arm, as we stood there looking at it.

"As of today, this is no longer Cold Stream for me," I said. "From now on it is The Lynching Stream."

THE END

Printed in the United States
16224LVS00005B/53